C000076689

Hidden Ink

Also from Carrie Ann Ryan

Redwood Pack Series
Book 1: *An Alpha's Path*
Book 2: *A Taste for a Mate*
Book 3: *Trinity Bound*
Book 3.5: *A Night Away*
Book 4: *Enforcer's Redemption*
Book 4.5: *Blurred Expectations*
Book 4.7: *Forgiveness*
Book 5: *Shattered Emotions*
Book 6: *Hidden Destiny*
Book 6.5: *A Beta's Haven*
Book 7: *Fighting Fate*
Book 7.5: *Loving the Omega*
Book 7.7: *The Hunted Heart*
Book 8: *Wicked Wolf*

The Talon Pack (Following the Redwood Pack)
Book 1: *Tattered Loyalties*
Book 2: *An Alpha's Choice*
Book 3: *Mated in Mist*

The Redwood Pack Volumes
Redwood Pack Vol 1
Redwood Pack Vol 2
Redwood Pack Vol 3
Redwood Pack Vol 4
Redwood Pack Vol 5
Redwood Pack Vol 6

Montgomery Ink
Book 0.5: *Ink Inspired*
Book 0.6: *Ink Reunited*
Book 1: *Delicate Ink*
The Montgomery Ink Box Set #1 (Contains Books 0.5, 0.6, 1)

Book 1.5: *Forever Ink (also found in Hot Ink)*
Book 2: *Tempting Boundaries*
Book 4: *Harder than Words*
Book 4: *Written in Ink*
Book 4.5: *Hidden Ink*
Book 5: Ink Enduring (Coming Jun 2016)

Dante's Circle Series
Book 1: *Dust of My Wings*
Book 2: *Her Warriors' Three Wishes*
Book 3: *An Unlucky Moon*
The Dante's Circle Box Set (Contains Books 1-3)
Book 3.5: *His Choice*
Book 4: *Tangled Innocence*
Book 5: *Fierce Enchantment*
Book 6: *An Immortal's Song (Coming April 2016)*
Book 7: *Prowled Darkness (Coming May 2016)*

Branded Packs (Written with Alexandra Ivy)
Book 1: *Stolen and Forgiven*
Book 2: *Abandoned and Unseen*
Book 3: *Buried and Shadowed (Coming July 2016)*

Holiday, Montana Series
Book 1: *Charmed Spirits*
Book 2: *Santa's Executive*
Book 3: *Finding Abigail*
The Holiday Montana Box Set (Contains Books 1-3)
Book 4: *Her Lucky Love*
Book 5: *Dreams of Ivory*

A Stand Alone Contemporary Romance
Finally Found You

Hidden Ink

A Montgomery Ink Novella

By Carrie Ann Ryan

1001 Dark Nights

EVIL EYE

CONCEPTS

Hidden Ink
A Montgomery Ink Novella
By Carrie Ann Ryan

1001 Dark Nights

Copyright 2016 Carrie Ann Ryan
ISBN: 978-1-942299-00-4

Foreword: Copyright 2014 M. J. Rose

Published by Evil Eye Concepts, Incorporated

All rights reserved. No part of this book may be reproduced, scanned, or distributed in any printed or electronic form without permission. Please do not participate in or encourage piracy of copyrighted materials in violation of the author's rights.

This is a work of fiction. Names, places, characters and incidents are the product of the author's imagination and are fictitious. Any resemblance to actual persons, living or dead, events or establishments is solely coincidental.

Acknowledgments

I am so grateful to be able to write the worlds I love and work with 1001 Dark Nights again. Thank you Liz Berry, MJ Rose, Kim, and Jillian, as well as the rest of the 1001 Dark Nights team!

This book and the characters inside hold a special place in my heart. I had hoped to write Hailey and Sloane's story almost two years ago, but the timing never truly worked out. Now it's finally time for them to find their HEA as well as for you readers to be able to see what secrets Hailey and Sloane hold.

Diving into Hailey's, as well as Sloane's, past made me look into myself more than I was ready for, but I am truly blessed that everyone will be able to read their story.

I want to thank Kennedy Layne, Shayla Blake, Carly Phillips, Lexi Blake, Angel Payne, and Julie Kenner for helping me along with this book. Writing it broke me ever so slightly.

And as always, thank you readers, for being with me for each step of my journey. You guys rock!

Sign up for the 1001 Dark Nights Newsletter
and be entered to win a Tiffany Key necklace.

There's a contest every month!

Go to www.1001DarkNights.com to subscribe.

As a bonus, all subscribers will receive a free
1001 Dark Nights story
The First Night
by Lexi Blake & M.J. Rose

One Thousand And One Dark Nights

Once upon a time, in the future…

*I was a student fascinated with stories and learning.
I studied philosophy, poetry, history, the occult, and
the art and science of love and magic. I had a vast
library at my father's home and collected thousands
of volumes of fantastic tales.*

*I learned all about ancient races and bygone
times. About myths and legends and dreams of all
people through the millennium. And the more I read
the stronger my imagination grew until I discovered
that I was able to travel into the stories... to actually
become part of them.*

*I wish I could say that I listened to my teacher
and respected my gift, as I ought to have. If I had, I
would not be telling you this tale now.
But I was foolhardy and confused, showing off
with bravery.*

*One afternoon, curious about the myth of the
Arabian Nights, I traveled back to ancient Persia to
see for myself if it was true that every day Shahryar
(Persian: شهريار, "king") married a new virgin, and then
sent yesterday's wife to be beheaded. It was written
and I had read, that by the time he met Scheherazade,
the vizier's daughter, he'd killed one thousand
women.*

Something went wrong with my efforts. I arrived in the midst of the story and somehow exchanged places with Scheherazade – a phenomena that had never occurred before and that still to this day, I cannot explain.

Now I am trapped in that ancient past. I have taken on Scheherazade's life and the only way I can protect myself and stay alive is to do what she did to protect herself and stay alive.

Every night the King calls for me and listens as I spin tales. And when the evening ends and dawn breaks, I stop at a point that leaves him breathless and yearning for more. And so the King spares my life for one more day, so that he might hear the rest of my dark tale.

As soon as I finish a story... I begin a new one... like the one that you, dear reader, have before you now.

Chapter One

Hailey Monroe bit into her lip, closed her eyes, and moaned. Loudly. Dear gods and goddesses that was…heavenly. Earth shattering. World changing. Orgasm inducing.

That was the best damn cream cheese turtle brownie she'd ever baked in her life.

She may have baked pies, cakes, tortes, cookies, muffins, biscotti, and other kinds of decadence in her past. But right now, with this beautiful, mouthwatering cream cheese turtle brownie in hand, she knew she'd never achieve such greatness again.

At that depressing thought, she ate the last of her treat and frowned.

Seriously? The pinnacle of her success in life, the greatness she had hoped to achieve lay in a brownie.

A brownie sent from heaven, mind you, but a brownie nonetheless.

She quickly wiped up any spare crumbs then went to the sink to wash her hands. It was kind of upsetting that in her twenty-seven years of living, this baking achievement was *it* for her. Most people would think finding a cure for the common cold, painting something that reaffirmed beauty and life for others, or building homes for the unfortunate would be something that made a pinnacle a pinnacle. Instead, Hailey had dessert. This divine brownie.

It probably didn't help her thoughts that she kept calling the damn thing heaven-sent and divine. It was just a baked good, one that crumbled when roughly handled, like the rest of them. It would be consumed wholly and forgotten in the next moment, never to be heard from again.

At least Hailey herself was stronger than that. Some days.

She cracked her knuckles, wincing at the pain in her joints—a *wonderful* side effect of all the drugs and treatments she'd poured into her system over the years—and rolled her neck. Today was a new day, a new adventure. It was the same mantra she repeated to herself every morning.

Hailey owned and operated Taboo, a café and bakery in the middle of downtown Denver. She had prime placement right off the 16th Street Mall and the business district. During prime hours, she had men and women in suits and neatly pressed clothes, begging for coffee and leaving with something sweet and delicious. No one could rightly say no to Hailey and her baked goods if she were really trying.

Her shop catered to more than just those in a hurry on their way to a meeting or working on a very important case. Families came in on late afternoons or on non-school days with children in tow. Her hot cocoa and cookies went quickly when school holidays met cold Denver weather days.

People in all shapes and sizes ventured into her shop, and she loved it. There was never a dull moment. Even when the place was only filled with a customer or two, they were *hers*. After thinking she'd never see the middle of her twenties, she was now looking at the back end of those years and owned her own business besides. She was a caretaker, a businesswoman, a baker…a survivor.

She pressed her lips together at the last word.

A survivor.

If she kept telling herself that, kept letting the news and random websites tell her more of the same, then one day she might believe it. However, she hated that word and everything that came with it. She'd fought and won, but at what cost?

Hailey shook her head. There was no time for those kinds of

thoughts this early February morning. Today, she had to make sure she was at least competing with the chain coffee shops around her—the Mega Starbucks two blocks over on each side of Taboo. Seriously, Denver had a Starbucks on every other corner, and where there wasn't a Starbucks, there was a Caribou Coffee or something else of the like. It wasn't as if she'd ever make as much money as them, but she did well. Her goal wasn't to become a millionaire or turn her small shop into a chain—she just wanted to *live*.

That's all she ever wanted to do.

So she'd compete in her own little way and make sure her shop looked ready for the next holiday. Valentine's Day. It was almost here. Actually, the clock calendar had just changed to February at midnight. Her decorated cookies and cupcakes would have hearts and pink all over them, and that morning, she'd put out her best festive Valentine's Day decorations. It wasn't overboard or cheesy, but just enough pink to remind her of happiness and love—not the pink that became an overbearing reminder in October.

Hell. Twice in one morning. She needed to stop being depressed about the past and look to her future with the same wide-eyed wonder she had as a teenager. Her aching bones and muscles could use the happiness.

Hailey rolled her shoulders back and finished up her morning prep. She'd been at it since four thirty that morning. Baker's hours were evil, but she didn't have to wake up as early as others, she knew. Her store opened at six a.m., and it was almost that time now. She had two people who worked for her, but Hailey was the one who did the baking and most of the cooking. The others worked the register and served while they were here. They also helped build the sandwiches or paninis—depending on the special on any given day—and heated the soups. Hailey made sure there was never a dull moment in Taboo.

The door between her shop and the one next door opened, and she pressed a hand to her stomach.

"I smelled coffee," Callie said as she walked in, her red-streaked black hair looking shiny that morning. In fact, the woman herself glowed. Her ink stood out on pale brown skin, and she smiled as if she had the best news in the world.

Considering Callie was six weeks pregnant, Hailey supposed she did.

"You scared the crap out of me," Hailey said with a laugh and rubbed her stomach again. She remembered the time when she used to rub the space over her heart if she was nervous or freaked out, but that was a long time ago.

Callie winced and bit into her dark ruby lip. "Sorry about that. I got to Montgomery Ink early to work on a sketch and needed coffee."

Hailey frowned and went to the coffee pot that she'd turned on only a few moments before. "I'm only giving you decaf. I don't want your very sexy, silver fox of a husband getting all growly with me. While you might like it when he gets growly with you because you get a spanking and orgasm out of it, I do not."

Callie pouted. "Fine. Decaf. Maybe I can trick my body into thinking it's real so I can pep up."

Hailey raised a brow as Callie bounced from foot to foot. "Honey, if you're any more pepped, you'll pep the heck out of Maya and Austin when they get into the shop."

Callie rolled her eyes before looking around Taboo. "Oh, I love when you decorate for a new season and holiday. You know how to do it so it's not all crepe paper and hearts dangling from the ceiling."

Hailey started the pot of decaf and held back a yawn. Maybe she needed some caffeine herself. With a sigh, she poured herself a cup of the regular coffee and set to work adding creamer, whipped cream, and chocolate shavings. It might not be an espresso since she didn't want to bother making that from scratch just then, but she could still have fun with the toppings.

"I don't mind the crepe paper and dangling hearts," Hailey said as she started work on Callie's decaf. With a little caramel and whipped cream, the sugar would help Callie feel like she was drinking the real thing. Plus, everything Hailey made was all-natural, so there wouldn't be any extra chemicals messing with the baby.

Callie took the offered cup with a smile. "My precious."

Hailey rolled her eyes. "Okay, Gollum. Drink up. And take a seat, okay? You're way too wired this morning, and yet you wanted caffeine. What's up?"

Callie sat and licked at her whipped cream. "I'm just happy, you know? This time two years ago I was just starting to work for Austin and the rest of the Montgomerys. Austin and Maya took a chance on me. And my sketches. Now I get to tattoo for a living. Plus, my Morgan was my first piece all on my own once Austin promoted me from apprentice to full-time artist. I not only got to ink the best phoenix in the world—because oh my God, have you seen his back? Heck, yeah—but I fell in love with him, too. And he loves me back, even though we're totally not the same age, and I say totally way too much. Now we're married and having a baby! It's unreal." Callie smiled big, her eyes bright. "Sometimes I feel like I don't deserve it. Like one day I'll wake up and everything will be just a dream and I'll be back working four jobs to pay rent on my ramshackle home. And Morgan won't be beside me every morning. He's my everything, and yet he shows me how to be *more* than that somehow."

Tears filled Callie's eyes and Hailey quickly handed over a few napkins. Her heart ached for some reason when it should have been only happy for the other woman. She and Callie were close in age, yet they had gone down such different paths that some days Hailey felt years older. The two of them and Miranda—Austin and Maya's youngest sister—were the youngest of the crew that hung out together. The Montgomerys and their circle ranged in age from mid-twenties to early forties, and most days, the age differences didn't matter. Hell, Morgan was in his forties and having a baby with Callie.

Age was just a number.

It was the heart and experience of a person that made things work.

Hailey didn't have her soul mate, didn't have that person who would help her find the better Hailey. She only had herself and her drive to keep going. That had to count for something. And she would *not* be jealous of Callie.

Just because Callie had met the man she was meant to be with and the man actually felt the same way about it didn't mean that Hailey wouldn't.

Of course, Hailey felt like she had already met that man, but that was neither here nor there. That man didn't want her so it was all water under the bridge anyway. What mattered at the moment was Callie and her tears, not whatever the hell was going on in Hailey's head.

Hailey pushed thoughts of sexy tattooed men who didn't want her out of her mind and went around the counter to put her arms around Callie.

"Honey, what's wrong?"

"I'm happy," Callie hiccupped. "Oh, God. I'm only in my first trimester and the hormones are getting me. How is that possible? I thought the tears and mood swings came in the third trimester and then right after the baby came."

Hailey kissed the top of Callie's dark hair and sighed. "I think it depends on the person. I've never been pregnant before so I don't know. You can ask Sierra or Meghan, though." Sierra was Austin's wife and Meghan was his sister. The two women were also part of Hailey's and Callie's inner circle. "They've been through all of this before. Meghan twice in fact. And who knows, with the way she and Luc are trying, she could get pregnant any day now and only be a couple months behind you."

"That would be nice," Callie said as she sniffed. The other woman wiped her face with the extra napkins Hailey had handed her and sighed. "This is crazy. I came in here because I love you and because, hello, coffee, and now I'm all weepy."

"Welcome to being pregnant." Hailey may not have firsthand experience with pregnancy, but the treatments she'd had in the past caused similar hormonal fluctuations. One minute she'd be happy, smiling away, the next, sobbing uncontrollably before moving on to a rage she'd never felt before. The drugs might technically be out of her system, but if she wasn't careful, sometimes, she still went through those mood swings.

Hailey had kept her previous diagnosis and past hidden, so she couldn't tell Callie any of that. She didn't know why she hadn't spoken of it before. Well, she knew a little bit. Once someone said the word *cancer*, she would be stuck with the label for the rest of her life.

She wouldn't be Hailey, the woman with the platinum-blonde bob and red lips.

She wouldn't be Hailey, café owner and businesswoman.

She wouldn't be Hailey, the woman with secrets who had a connection to the sexy man next door, which no one spoke of but everyone knew existed.

She would become Hailey, breast cancer survivor.

Hailey, not whole.

Hailey, not fully a woman.

She mentally slapped herself. It had been how long, and she was still feeling this way? It had been years since the surgeries, the treatments. She was cancer free. Enough time had passed that she *was* cancer free, not just in remission.

Hailey wasn't the same woman she was before, but in all honesty, who was the same person they were at age twenty?

She needed to push that aside and worry about Callie right then. One day soon, she would tell the girls about her cancer. She hadn't known them when she was sick, but keeping secrets like this wore on her. Plus, she wanted to make sure the girls were taking care of themselves. She'd been young when she was diagnosed, way too young for that type of illness, and yet she'd had to go through everything that came with it. She didn't want her friends to face the same things she had.

No one deserved that.

"I'm happy," Callie said again, this time her eyes clear of tears.

"And Morgan is going to freak when he finds out that I cried today. Because even if you don't say anything. He'll know. He's just that good."

Hailey kissed her friend's cheek and let out a laugh. "It's because he loves you."

Oh, to be loved like that. Unconditionally. To know that someone could see deep inside and know every emotion, and take the time—and care enough—to cradle that feeling...

Hailey was indeed jealous, but it didn't matter. Callie deserved all of that and more.

All of her friends did.

"He does love me, doesn't he?" Callie said with a smile. "Okay, now that I've gotten coffee out of you and cried on your shoulder, I'm going back to the shop to work like I said I would." She let out a sigh. "Another reason I'm in here early is that Morgan had a super early appointment. The call was with someone in another time zone. I hate being at home alone. So thank you for being you and letting me ramble. The guys and Maya should be into the shop a bit later. I'll send them over since those brownies look to die for."

Hailey grinned. "They *are* absolutely amazing. I taste-tested one this morning. For business purposes, of course."

"How you keep your curves looking like a fifties pinup *and* taste all of your sweets is beyond me."

Hailey snorted. "It takes a lot of yoga and running to keep me in the shape I am, thank you very much. And you're like the size of one of my legs, so shut up."

Callie rolled her eyes then bounced toward Montgomery Ink. Hailey loved the fact that there was a door between the two shops. When Hailey had first opened her shop four years ago, she'd been intimidated by the very broody, bearded, tattooed men next door. And then there was Maya.

The tattoo artist and middle Montgomery girl was a force to be reckoned with—all ink, piercings, and attitude. So, of course, Hailey became friends with her right away. Contrary to her feelings about being next door to people she hadn't quite understood at first, she fell in love with their connections, attitudes, and sense of family. They were loud when they wanted to be, quiet and respectful at other times. They partied when they felt like it and threw small gatherings other times. They weren't rough and tough to the point where she ever felt scared to be around them. Others might be assholes and judge the Montgomerys on their ink—and yes, their kink—but Hailey had found her soulmates. Her family.

She didn't have a family of her own so it was nice to be adopted into theirs, welcomed into their open arms. Though the door between the shops had been there before she bought the place, the Montgomerys hadn't used it with the prior owner— a prim and proper older woman who had no time for tattoos and ruffians.

Seriously. Her words.

Now the door was never locked, and the Montgomerys and their crew could come in and out of Taboo when they wanted food and caffeine. Hailey went over there often, as well, with trays of goodies and sometimes empty-handed just to see the beautiful artwork.

She was still a blank canvas, but knew she eventually wanted ink of her own.

One day she would be brave enough to ask for it.

It wasn't the ink she was afraid of, wasn't the needles. God knew she'd seen enough of those in her life thanks to chemo, radiation, and the countless tests and treatments.

No, it was the person she wanted to do her ink.

While Maya, Austin, and Callie would bend over backward to help her with her tattoo and the nerves that came with it, she didn't want them to do it. She had someone else in mind.

Someone she was afraid to talk to for fear of what would spill out.

Someone who didn't care for her as she cared for him.

Hailey's phone buzzed and she sighed. Today was a day for melancholy thoughts, apparently. She turned off the timer on her phone then went to the front of the café to flip the sign to *Open* while unlocking the door. Two of her morning regulars, men in business suits, who had the courtesy to get off their phones before they walked into the shop, smiled at her.

"Good morning, gentlemen," she said with a smile. "Your usuals?"

"You know it," one said.

"Of course," the other one added in.

She smiled widely then went back to her counter to get their drinks and pastries. Soon her help would be there to work the register so she wouldn't be alone. The crisp morning air had filtered in with the brief opening and closing of the door, and as she worked quickly, she knew today would be a good day.

Any day she could do what she loved would be a better day than the last.

By the time Corrine came in and took over the front station, Hailey was already buzzing with the adrenaline of a morning rush. There was nothing like earning a living doing something she loved. The brownies were a hit, and the first batch she'd set out was soon gone. Normally, she would have saved them for the afternoon crowd so customers would eat her bagels and other morning delights, but she didn't have the heart to hide them in the back. Nor did she have the will.

She'd have eaten the whole batch and gained all that weight Callie had joked about. Lying on the kitchen floor in a sugar coma wasn't the best way to run a bakery.

The morning passed by quickly, and soon, Hailey found herself in a slight lull. After talking to Corrine, she made a tray of pastries and to-go cups of coffee—each one individualized for someone special. She wasn't sure exactly who was working today over at Montgomery Ink, but she knew at least the main people would be there, and she was familiar with their drink of choice. Even if she made extra, nothing would go to waste. Austin and Maya would make sure of that.

Hailey made her way through the door and held back a sigh at the sound of needles buzzing and the deep voices of those speaking. She loved Montgomery Ink. It was part of her home.

"Caffeine! I want to have your babies. Can I have your babies, sexy momma?" Maya asked as she cradled her coffee and cheese pastry.

Hailey snorted. "Are you talking to me or the coffee?"

Maya blinked up at her, the ring in her brow glittering under the lights. "Yes."

Hailey just shook her head and handed off a drink to Austin, who bussed a kiss on her cheek. His beard tickled her, and once again, she wanted to bow down at Sierra's feet in jealousy. Seriously, the man was hot. All the Montgomerys were.

Soon she found herself with only one drink on her tray along with a single cherry and cream cheese pastry.

His favorite.

Behind Maya's work area sat another station.

Sloane Gordon's.

All six-foot-four, two hundred something pounds of muscle covered in ink, his light brown skin accented perfectly by the designs. The man was sex. All sex. Sloane had shaved his head years ago. She was convinced he kept it shaved just to turn her on. He kept his beard trimmed, but that and the bald head apparently jump-started a new kink in her.

Who knew?

He was a decade older than Hailey, and though he didn't speak of it, she knew he'd been through war, battle, and heartbreak.

And she loved him.

Only he didn't *see* her. He never took a step toward her. He also looked as if he were ready to growl at her presence most of the time.

Much like he did now.

"Thought you'd forgotten me," he said, his voice low and gruff.

She shook her head then raised her chin. "No, I have yours here." After she had handed him his drink and pastry, careful not to brush her fingers along his, she glanced down at his client, who was in the middle of getting his back done.

While Sloane looked dangerous and battle worn, this guy looked gentler, but not soft in the slightest. His hair was longer on top and flopped down over his forehead and into his eyes, but the sides had been clipped short. He had a short beard and a smile that looked as if it came easily. His green eyes sparkled, and Hailey could only smile back.

"Hello there," he drawled.

Oh, my. A southern accent—just a hint of drawl but not too much. If she hadn't been in the presence of the one man her body and soul had chosen for her, she might have gone weak in the knees at the sound of it.

"Hi," she said back, well aware that Sloane was staring daggers at her.

"What's your name?" the stranger asked. "I'm Brody."

"Hi, Brody. I'm Hailey. I own Taboo next door."

His smile widened, showing a bit of dimple. "I've walked by there a few times, but now I know I need to go inside."

She shook her head on a laugh. "I see. You scent my baked goods and now you'll come inside."

"It wasn't your baked goods that made me want to step inside."

What was she doing? Flirting with another man in front of Sloane like this? And why did she care? He wasn't hers. He never would be. She would never have Sloane Gordon in her life beyond a few curt words and grunts of thanks. She was young, healthy, and *alive*. She should be able to flirt whenever she wanted.

Determined not to look at Sloane, or notice how quiet it had gotten within Montgomery Ink, she tilted her head and put her hand on her hip.

"Really?" she asked.

"Really. How about I come over after I get this done and have a bit of sugar to keep me going?"

She laughed, throwing her head back. "Oh, honey, that was a terrible line, but you are welcome to come over. I'll give you a bit of…sugar." She winked then turned toward the door, adding a little sway to her hips as she left.

She might not be able to have the man she wanted, but she could still be *free*.

She wasn't the same woman she'd been before the cancer destroyed her body and soul, but she was still Hailey Monroe.

Strong.

Alive.

And annoyingly single.

Maybe it was time to do something about that. Sloane or no Sloane.

Chapter Two

Sloane Gordon forced his foot off the pedal and carefully, oh-so-carefully, set the tattoo gun on his counter. Permanently maiming the little fucker in his chair was bad for business. Plus, he didn't feel like going to jail for harming the shit. Sloane already looked like someone who had spent a few years behind bars—even if he hadn't. He didn't need to perpetuate the image.

But the man in front of him was *this* close to getting his ass kicked.

Who the fuck wore their hair like that? This kid looked like he was in a boy band and should be bouncing around on stage as teenage girls screamed his name. Sure, Brody looked to be around Hailey's age and was a *little* bigger in muscle than the kids who sang about lost loves and being theirs forever, but it was the principle of the matter.

No man should hit on a woman while she was working. Especially not when said woman was Hailey Monroe.

Sloane's Hailey.

Only she wasn't his. Contrary to popular belief, he'd never been with Hailey—though he'd thought about it. Often. He'd never held her in his arms, never cupped her cheek and felt the softness of her skin—because damn it, it would be soft. It just looked it. Soft and warm and perfect.

Hailey Monroe wasn't Sloane's, and he needed to get control of himself.

The two of them had a connection from the very first time they saw each other, but he'd never claimed her. Not that she was his to claim and all, but he'd stayed back. He knew she wasn't for him, or rather, *he* wasn't for *her*. So he'd done the best thing possible and stayed away.

That didn't mean he was okay with some new guy with too much product in his hair hitting on her. Of course, Sloane hadn't missed the way Hailey had flirted right back. She'd even moved her hips just enough while walking away to let them all know she was aware of being watched.

What the hell was up with that?

In the few years they'd been circling each other yet never moving closer, he hadn't once seen her go on a date, hadn't seen her flirt with another man beyond a wink or two. Those winks, he knew, were just her personality. But he wanted them all.

He was a selfish bastard and he didn't want her flirting with Brody. He didn't want to see her with another man period, especially not one she'd flirted with right in front of him.

What kind of man did that make Sloane?

He wanted her, but he couldn't be with her so he wouldn't let others be with her either.

He wasn't sure he liked that man, but hell, he couldn't stop himself. He could say he'd always been this way, but that would be a lie. He'd never reacted this way to another man around Hailey. But she'd never flirted back either. Sure, Griffin had joked about things with Hailey and she'd smiled in the past, but Griffin would never have crossed the line. Now he was with Autumn and no longer a concern when it came to Hailey.

There was an unwritten rule that Hailey was *his,* and he needed to figure out what he was going to do about it. He knew he didn't have the right to do anything about it, but that didn't stop him from dreaming, from wondering.

He looked up from his hands and into Austin Montgomery's

eyes. His boss raised a brow and looked worried. Sloane couldn't blame the other man. *He* wasn't quite sure what he was going to do. It wasn't Brody's fault that he'd stepped into something even Sloane didn't understand. That didn't mean Sloane was going to make it easy on the kid.

Sloane and Hailey had a dance of sorts that had been going on since day one. They'd get slightly closer, but then one or the other would back away. They'd talk about everything and nothing at the same time. She always left him the best cookies and made sure he was fed and taken care of no matter what. He always made sure she was safe, never letting her walk to her car out in the back parking lot alone. At social functions where they were together in a large group, they usually sat next to or near one another. They never touched, but they made sure they were always in the vicinity of each other.

The others knew that there was *something* between him and Hailey. Hell, the guys and Maya razzed him about it more often than not. It wasn't that Sloane was never going to make a move; it was that he wanted to make sure it was the right time for that move.

He blinked. Well, hell, that idea was new. Apparently, he *would* be making a move. He was barely in the right headspace most days, let alone in the right place for him to be with Hailey. He'd moved slow, wanting to ensure that he didn't spook her, didn't fuck himself over. Because when he did move—if that happened at all—there would be no turning back. He wanted to be her everything, much like she already was for him. She'd be his in body and truth, and he'd make sure he gave her what he could. There was no partway when it came to the ownership of his heart, his soul. But some darkness would have to remain his and his alone.

And until he could know for sure that the darkness within him wouldn't touch Hailey, he had to hold himself back. He'd known he was playing with fire by waiting, by watching for years and never doing more. But she'd held back, too. She'd known it wasn't the right time yet.

Or maybe he was wrong? Maybe he'd screwed up and now he

was about to lose it all. Lose it to someone closer to her age, someone who made her laugh and her eyes sparkle.

Sloane wanted to be the man that made her throw her head back and laugh like that. He wanted to be all of those things and more. But he couldn't. Not yet. It wasn't the time, and now it might not ever be the time.

Jesus, his head hurt from going back and forth. He wanted her, he ached for her, but he wasn't good enough for her. He'd never be pure for her. But at some point he may have to let that go. Realize that while he wasn't light—instead, darkness—he was still *hers*. And that would have to be sufficient.

Sloane might not be good enough for Hailey, but damn it, nobody was. This Brody, with his too-gelled hair, wasn't even close to being what she needed.

"Are we taking a break?" Brody asked as he looked over his shoulder. "Everything looking good back there?"

Maya cleared her throat, and Sloane forced his attention away from Brody and toward the other tattoo station. His other boss and friend pressed her lips together, surprising him. He'd have thought Maya would have a sarcastic quip or something to say about what the hell had just happened. Even Callie stood by Maya's side, wide-eyed and a little surprised. He didn't blame the younger woman. For as long as he'd known her, she'd been trying to figure out why he wasn't with Hailey.

How was he supposed to tell them he wasn't worthy of the blonde bombshell with secrets of her own? That if he was with her, he'd taint the beauty of her soul, the exquisiteness of her smile. That's what he did. He brought in the shadows, carved deep inside, and rotted the core of someone because of what he'd done, what he'd seen.

But he was a selfish bastard. He knew that. Sloane knew it might be time for him to stand up and actually do something about what he'd been hiding from for years. To do that, however, he needed to make sure this kid knew his place.

"Shit," Brody mumbled under his breath. "I stepped in it, didn't I?" The younger man turned slightly in his chair and grimaced. "I didn't know she was yours, bro. I just saw a pretty girl with no ring on her finger and thought she was fair game. I'm sorry. I didn't know she was taken."

Sloane let out a breath, his rage over this kid backing down slightly, though the swirl of self-pity was well on the rise. Lovely.

"She's not…"

Brody shook his head. "Yeah, she is. I saw the way you looked at her, and I know you're about this close to knocking my head right off my shoulders. So you might not be dating her officially, but I stepped in it. I'll go in there and then back off. I'd just leave, but that wouldn't be right, and I don't want to hurt her feelings. You know?" He shrugged. "If you don't want to finish my ink, I get it."

Sloane was aware that the others were staring at him, waiting for him to confirm or deny his so-called relationship with Hailey. They were waiting for him to say something. Anything.

"I'm not going to fuck up your ink, kid."

Brody raised a brow. "I know I'm taking my life in my hands, but I'm not that much younger than you. No need to call me kid."

Maya muttered something under her breath about insolent fools while Austin groaned.

"You're asking for me to punch you in the face, aren't you?" Sloane growled out, his voice low and deep. Though in reality, his voice was always low and deep.

"Not really. I just figured if you're calling *me* kid and Hailey looked to be about the same age as me, then maybe you're calling *her* kid, as well."

"Jesus Christ," Austin growled. The man also coughed out what suspiciously sounded like a chuckle.

"How about you shut up and let me finish your ink?" Sloane asked casually, though he felt anything but casual. "Then you can head on out of here and we'll call it a day."

Brody sighed then turned so Sloane could work on the last

shading of the tattoo. "Whatever, Sloane. But I've got to say, if Hailey smiled at me like that, maybe you need to step up your game and actually do something about her. Because if you're saying that you're not with her but act like no one else can be with her either, that might cause problems. Just saying."

"Brody, for the love of God, stop talking," Maya snapped. "He has a tattoo gun like two inches from your skin. Do you really want to piss him off?"

"He's not going to mess up my ink," Brody said back slowly. "He already said that."

"I might change my mind," Sloane said. He wouldn't. None of the crew at Montgomery Ink would. Even pissed off, they wouldn't fuck up ink. That was their income, their passion, their life. Fucking up ink was not an option.

"You wouldn't," Brody said calmly. "You like me, even if you want to punch me in the face right now."

Sloane chuckled slowly and he saw Austin's shoulders relax at the sound. "Hell, kid, you have an ego on you."

"Helps with the ladies. Though not your lady. I won't poach."

If Sloane hadn't wanted to kick this kid's ass for daring to come near Hailey, he might have become friends with the idiot. As it was, he was withholding judgment on that until he could figure out what the hell he was going to do about Hailey at all. He couldn't keep doing this, couldn't keep freaking out if another man came near her. Of course, he hadn't actually freaked out physically before. This was a first.

She'd smiled at Brody.

She'd given him one of *Sloane's* smiles.

Hell. He needed to get his head out of his ass.

He finished up Brody's work in silence then stretched his back as the other guy stood up and ran a hand through his hair.

"Okay, I'm going to go tell Hailey I won't be by later. That way I don't make her feel like shit or something, you know?"

Sloane just raised an eyebrow. "You told her you were going to stop by after you were done with your ink. It's after your ink, so you stopping by to go in there to tell her you won't be stopping by seems kind of idiotic."

Brody just shrugged. "You not doing anything about a woman you clearly have feelings for seems idiotic."

"Oh, dear God," Maya mumbled, and Austin let out a rough chuckle.

"Shut it, Montgomerys," Sloane bit out. Freaking Montgomery clan, always getting in his business.

"The kid's not wrong," Austin said quietly. "You've been circling around that girl for years. If you're not going to do something about it, maybe it's time to back off."

Sloane let out a low growl and narrowed his eyes at his one-time friend. Austin stared back, unrepentant. Sloane flipped him off then brought his attention back to Brody.

"Why don't you just go and I'll deal with Hailey?"

Brody's brows rose. "And if I choose to go in there so she doesn't think I'm an asshole?"

Sloane snarled, and Brody raised his hands in surrender. "Hell, Sloane. Fine, but you better go in there and make sure she doesn't feel like I didn't come in because of her. You get me? Because that's a shitty thing to do."

"I'll make sure she understands." Not that he understood. What the hell was he doing anyway? Now he was pushing men out of Hailey's way and acting like a complete idiot. He'd have to go over there and talk to her about feelings and shit. Sure, they talked about everything under the sun that had nothing to do with what was important usually, but he had a feeling this would be important.

Why the hell was he changing things?

Why the hell had she said yes to Brody?

Brody tilted his head. "You know what, screw it. I'm going over there to tell her I won't be by for sugar. I'm not going to be the asshole here. You are."

Sloane wanted to reach out and grab the kid by the neck, but he restrained himself. The other man walked through the door connecting Montgomery Ink and Taboo, leaving Sloane feeling like an idiot of epic proportions.

"I can't believe you just did that," Callie said softly. "I know you and Hailey have this...thing or whatever, but you seriously just stepped in it."

"Don't start with me, Callie."

"Don't get mad at the pregnant chick," Maya snapped.

This time, it was Sloane who held up his hands in surrender. "Jesus. What the hell is wrong with everyone today?"

Maya stalked toward him, her eyebrow ring glittering under the lights. "Oh, I don't know, maybe it's because we're watching you act like a douche and yet you don't seem to see it."

He ran his tongue over his teeth. Oh, he knew he was being a douche, but he didn't know how to stop it. He hadn't been able to stop many things recently, and yet he just kept making mistakes. Kept getting closer and closer to Hailey, knowing he'd be the one to hurt her eventually. He'd stayed away from her for a reason at first, then made sure to keep his feelings in check when he hadn't been able to be away anymore.

Now he'd put himself in the center of something that was rightly none of his business. A small part of him didn't care, and that part wanted her to be his until the end of days. But the rational part of his mind knew he needed to stay away. It would be better for everyone if he just kept to himself and kept Hailey on her side of the wall.

But he'd fucked that up.

Truly.

"You're not going to say anything?" Maya asked. She searched his face, and this time, he didn't see anger, he saw disappointment. Nothing cut him quicker than seeing that in the eyes of his friends. "I want you happy, Sloane. Why can't you see that?"

"I could say the same about you," he said without thinking.

Her eyes widened for a moment, her face paling. "You know what? The hell with it. I'm done. Hurt yourself, block off any emotion you think you could have, but if you hurt Hailey any more than you already have, I'll kick you in the balls."

With that, she stormed off, and he closed his eyes, cursing himself. Maya had her own issues and he shouldn't have brought it up, even in the vaguest of senses. Friends didn't do that, didn't dig the knife deeper when they knew the other was hurting.

Yet Sloane kept messing things up.

"Why don't you go for a walk or go sketch?" Austin asked quietly. "Take a breather."

Sloane let out a breath and gave a tight nod. Montgomery Ink was his family, and he had to remember that. He'd been dancing around what Hailey meant to him, what he wanted her to mean to him, for far too long, and now he had to deal with the consequences. The others had always known there might be something brewing between the two of them, but now he'd done something blatant about that...connection.

And as soon as Hailey found out about what he'd done, he'd be in for it.

He closed the office door behind him and let out a sigh, running a hand over his face. Then he sat down at the main desk and traced his finger over the edge of his sketchbook. He'd been an artist for as long as he could remember, though he'd never thought of himself as such. He'd been good with a pencil since he'd been a kid and yet had always held it close to the vest. He hadn't wanted the others to know what he could do. Not when a weakness such as art could mean a fist.

He'd learned long ago that his fingers were better for triggers than graphite and ink.

Or so his father had told him.

His skin tightened and he clenched his jaw, forcing his breath to come in even pants rather than the shallow ones his lungs seemed to want to do. His chest constricted and he rubbed his fist over his heart.

He stuck his ear buds in his ears and turned on some alt-rock that didn't have too much bass and had the lead singer's soothing croons instead of lyrical whining about lost hearts and lack of empathy. Sloane needed to calm down before he had another anxiety attack. He'd never had one in the middle of the shop, but he'd been damn close before. It'd been a decade since he'd been in the service, and yet he could still hear the yells, the shots that never seemed to go away. If he took deep breaths and focused on drawing, he could calm himself enough that he wouldn't break out in a cold sweat. If he beat back the pain, he wouldn't vomit on the floor, wouldn't smash his hand into the drywall because he didn't know another form of release.

Sloane nodded to the beat as he forced his eyes open. His hands once again traced the sketchbook before he opened it, pencil in hand. He had a few drawings to finish so they were ready for clients, as well as things on his mind he could just draw for relaxation, but his mind wouldn't focus.

Couldn't focus.

A hand touched his shoulder and he whirled around, standing in one breath, his hand raised, the pencil poised as a weapon. The beat of the music increased, as did the sound of his heart.

Hailey stood in front of him, her eyes wide, one hand on her chest, the other out in front of her.

Protecting herself.

From him.

This was why he wasn't for her.

This was why he'd stayed away.

He'd only hurt her. Only lose her to the demons that plagued him.

"What?" he bit out, pulling the ear buds from his ears.

She took a step back at the sound of his voice.

Sloane let out a breath. "Shit. I didn't mean to scare you. You just startled me."

Her throat worked as she swallowed hard. "I can see that." She licked her lips and put her hands down, fisting them at her sides.

"What the hell is wrong with you?"

He froze, not knowing what to say. Had she seen the panic in his gaze? Seen the fact that he wasn't whole? That he was damaged goods…far too broken for a woman like her?

"Why did Brody tell me to 'take it up with Sloane' when he said he wasn't interested in me?" she continued.

He swallowed hard, the short burst of relief that she hadn't seen the truth of him quickly replaced with the damning feeling he'd messed up.

"He wasn't good enough for you," he said simply.

Her eyes narrowed, her cheeks pinking with color. He loved the way her face carried emotion. Most of the time she kept her smile on, as if she had to be happy and bubbly for her clients, adding "sugars" to her drawl when she felt like it. But sometimes he saw beneath that, saw the woman he wanted in his life but knew he couldn't have.

"Fuck you, Sloane."

His brows rose. Hailey didn't normally curse at him.

"Don't look at me like that, you asshole. In fact, don't look at me at all. Who do you think you are? Who the hell do you think you are, Sloane? I thought you were my friend, but maybe I was wrong. What kind of man steps in and tells another to back off? It wasn't your place, that's for sure. I smiled at *one* man. That's it. I said I'd be over at my shop when he was through with his ink. That's it. And yet, that somehow triggered your alpha complex and you had to scare him away. How dare you say he's not good enough for me? You don't know him. And, apparently, you sure as hell don't know me."

Tears filled her eyes and she blinked them back quickly, raising her chin.

Damn it. He was an ass. A prick. A loser. A douche.

"Why did you do it?" she asked, her voice low. "You've stayed away from me for *years*. We've been friends but never got too close. Why did you change the rules?"

She'd changed them first by flirting with a man in front of him, but he didn't bring that up. He'd already hurt her, hurt himself in the process.

He needed to man up, he knew it, but he also knew he really wasn't good enough for her—wasn't what she needed.

"I'll take you out," he said, surprising himself.

Her jaw dropped. "What?"

"Go out to dinner with me." What the hell was he doing? He'd pushed Brody away because he thought the guy wasn't good enough for her—or so he told himself—but that didn't mean Sloane *was* good enough for her. In fact, he knew he wasn't.

"You told Brody to go away because you wanted to go out with me?" she asked, her voice rising.

"You said I changed the rules, so let's change them more. Go out with me."

She blinked rapidly then nodded. "Fine."

Not the best response, but he'd screwed the asking up royally. He couldn't blame her. "I'll pick you up at seven."

"Tonight? You want to go out tonight?"

"You have a problem with that?" Could he be more of an ass?

"You know what? I don't know anymore, Sloane. I have no idea what's going on, but fine. I'll see you at seven." She let out a breath, closed her eyes for a beat, and then met his gaze. "I hope we figure out what we're doing before it's too late." She whispered the last part before walking out of the office, leaving him alone.

He hoped for their sake they figured it out as well. Because he'd just crashed through the wall they'd carefully erected between the two of them, and now they'd have to deal with the consequences.

And while his mind whirled and he tried to figure out what the next step would be, that small part of him that always held out hope, the part he knew he buried deep daily, pulsated.

He was going out with Hailey.

Finally.

And he was going to mess it all up. Again. It was what he did. He just prayed he didn't break Hailey in the process.

Chapter Three

Hailey had lost her damn mind. That was the only explanation for why she was standing in front of her mirror in her robe with her hands wringing in front of her. It all seemed like a dream, but from the way her heart beat in her chest, she knew it was real.

Far too real.

One minute she'd been making coffee, trying to figure out how she'd get out of drinks or whatever with Brody, and the next she was standing in Sloane's office saying yes to a date. With *him*.

It didn't make sense.

The moment she'd stepped back into her café, she'd known she made a mistake flirting with Brody. While she'd wanted to stand up and take a step in a direction that didn't include her waiting for a man who would never truly want her, she hadn't meant to take a leap that fast. It wasn't that Brody wasn't attractive. And he'd been sweet to her. It was more that he wasn't *for* her. And while, at the time, she'd thought Sloane would never be for her either, she knew she didn't want Brody like that. It had been a lapse in judgment and one she would have had to fix right away.

Only Brody had shown up all apologetic smiles, saying he wouldn't be staying. While she should have felt hurt that he would back out so quickly, she could only feel relief. He seemed like a nice guy—with perhaps a dangerous edge—but she didn't want him the way she should. Even for a cup of coffee with a bit of flirtation. She'd smiled back and said she understood—though she hadn't truly understood his quick change of mind, even if she'd been relieved. When she'd asked him if there was anything wrong, he'd told her to ask Sloane about it, and she'd had to clutch the sides of the counter, hard.

After dropping that bomb, the damn man had just walked out of her café, hands in his pockets with a smile on his face.

It didn't make sense. Why would Sloane have anything to do with Brody backing out of their almost-date? So, when she'd stormed over to Montgomery Ink, angry and hurt that Sloane would dare to interfere, especially when he hadn't done anything when it came to her and him—at all—she'd been ready to tear him a new one.

No one had been more surprised than her when he'd asked her out.

Or rather, when he'd told her they were going out.

She wasn't quite sure how it had happened, only that she'd raised her chin and said yes. She shouldn't have, she knew. The man hadn't wanted her until someone else had taken a chance. That wasn't how relationships were supposed to start. He wasn't supposed to keep her at arm's length, waiting for him to make up his mind. That wasn't fair to her, wasn't fair to him.

And yet she'd been weak.

She'd said *yes.*

She closed her eyes as she gripped the edges of her robe. There was no way Hailey could back out now. He'd be there to pick her up soon, and then she'd take another chance at life.

She'd taken that chance before—had the scars to prove it—so maybe she could do this. Maybe she could be with someone and remember that it wasn't the wholeness of her body that made her who she was, but the strength of what was inside. Only, she'd proven she was weak by saying yes in the first place, hadn't she? She'd given in to his actions to get them where they were too easily.

She was so damn confused, and the fact that she was *excited* at the same time didn't help. She'd wanted Sloane for years, and now they were getting their chance. Maybe she should just push aside the *how* and go with the *now*.

Hailey opened her eyes and met her gaze in the mirror. She could live in the now—she'd been doing it since that fateful day when she'd faced her mortality with a fragile strength she hadn't known she possessed. Oh, she and Sloane would have to discuss how it had come to be, if only for a few moments, but she could move on.

She fingered the edge of the robe before letting the fabric fall to the floor. She stood naked in front of her mirror, relying on a strength she had long since honed in the darkness.

Her surgeon had done a wonderful job, but there was only so much anyone could do with a bilateral mastectomy that dug deep into the tissues. It had taken six surgeries for her reconstructive surgeon to find the right balance. Each time, she'd cried in pain, threw up from the meds, and ached in places so deep she never thought she'd be able to get up and breathe again.

Her breasts were gone.

What remained was thanks to the skill of her surgeon. A large scar—slightly faded over time but there nonetheless—slashed through each new breast. Other scars from surgeries, ports, and treatments covered her upper chest, her belly, and between her breasts. It wasn't pretty, and sometimes she knew it was downright horrific.

When she'd first taken off the bindings and pads from the initial surgery, she'd sobbed—gut wrenching sobs that wracked her whole body...or at least the body that remained. They hadn't been able to start the reconstructive process until her second surgery due to the depth of her cancer cells. It shouldn't have hurt her as much as it had. She was *alive*. Breasts were just breasts.

But that was all a fucking lie.

She was a *woman*. Her breasts had been part of her. She'd loved her body, even as a twenty-year-old. Sure, she might have wanted slightly more curves where it mattered when she'd been that young, but it hadn't happened. Instead of coming into her own out of her teens, she'd faced her own mortality in a way no woman should have to.

So, yes, to the outside world she had a normal body—if normal was even a word these days. Her surgeon had been brilliant, and after all these years, Hailey knew how to wear the right clothes to ensure no one would guess what scars lay beneath.

But she wasn't the same woman she'd once been.

One thing she'd done differently than most women was her nipples. She'd opted to not have them kept in any sense of the word, as some women do. It hadn't been the right surgery for her, and she'd wanted to move on. Her nipples weren't part of who she was—or at least that's what she'd thought at first. She'd also decided not to do anything about tattooing fake ones on. At least not yet. She'd warred with herself over it and had even almost asked Maya to do it for her…but it wasn't what she wanted. She'd had implants put in during one of the later surgeries, though they weren't perfectly even. She'd missed her curves, and though at the time the new ones hadn't felt like *hers*, she'd grown to see them differently.

In the years since her diagnosis and recovery, she'd formulated a plan. She wanted a certain kind of tattoo over what were once her breasts, and in her heart, she knew whom she wanted to do it. While Maya, Austin, or Callie would take great care of her, she wanted the one person she knew carried a darkness, a scar along his soul as deep, if not deeper, than her physical ones.

She wanted Sloane.

She let out a shuddered breath.

She'd never had the courage to ask him…maybe it was time. After all, if he saw her naked, he'd know about her breasts. And if she took this date—this relationship—further, he'd see it all.

It was a step she hadn't been willing to take before, but maybe, just maybe, Brody's interference would help her not only heal the remaining scars on her body, her *soul*, but show Sloane what he could have with her—what she could have with him.

She wasn't the woman she once was, she reminded herself, but then again, no one truly was.

With a roll of her shoulders, she donned her dark leggings and tunic top. It clung just right to her curves but didn't showcase any unevenness in her chest. No matter how many surgeries she had, she'd never have perfect globes. Then again, she hadn't when they'd been real anyway. Bras and holding her shoulders back helped with those issues. Once she was naked...well, that was another form of trust, one that she'd tried to give before but failed.

A year or so after her last surgery, she'd slept with a man she'd been seeing. He'd known she had cancer, but hadn't known the depth of her...newness. He hadn't made her come during the encounter, and had stayed away from her upper chest to the point she felt like a pariah. She couldn't get the sensations she'd once had with nipple play since she didn't have them anymore, but completely ignoring where they once had been by not even glancing at them when she'd had her shirt off had quickly ruined any tingling she might have felt for the man. Part of that may have been her fault as she hadn't communicated her feelings, but damn it, he should have tried to make things better for her.

She hadn't slept with a man since.

The fact that it took her longer with a vibrator to come than it had before the chemo and radiation didn't make things any easier. But if she were patient—and honest about thinking about Sloane while getting herself off—she could come eventually. And while she missed hot sex, she missed the intimacy of being with another even more. She'd had a few boyfriends during high school and the start of college, so she hadn't been that inexperienced. She also hadn't had a boyfriend during the ordeal, so she'd gone from who she'd been to this new version of her without someone to see the progress.

Going out with Sloane tonight was a hurdle of trust she'd never faced before...at least a different type of one. If and when she told him about her cancer, told him of her body, she'd be giving a part of herself to him—an intimate part—before she even let him touch her.

She trusted Sloane more than she trusted almost anyone—just from the way he'd treated her since they met. The chemistry between them had only burned brighter as time moved on.

They both had their reasons for keeping away until now.

She would tell him hers because there would be no hiding it if things progressed.

She just hoped he'd tell her his.

"Enough of that," she mumbled to herself. She'd spent the past twenty minutes staring in the mirror, trying to figure out how she'd gotten herself into this situation, and now she was going to be late if she didn't get a move on.

As fast as she could, she finished straightening her hair, the sleek threads forming a perfect bob. Her post chemo hair wasn't as straight as it used to be so she had to iron out the wave if she wanted her hairstyle to work. Her thick bangs rocked in her opinion, and she was grateful her hair hadn't thinned like so many others' had. This hairstyle, actually, came from one of the wigs she'd had during her treatments. She'd loved the way it framed her face so much, she'd let her hair grow out into the style.

She quickly did her makeup, making sure her lips were stained a deep red. If she pressed a glass to her lips or even kissed Sloane later, the stain wouldn't come off. She loved this brand and prayed her shop continued to do well so she could afford it.

The knock on the door came precisely on time, and she grinned. Sloane was known for his promptness. And knowing him and his military mindset, he had probably been outside for five minutes waiting for her because being right on time was actually late to him. She wasn't usually late for things, but she sometimes came in by the skin of her teeth.

Hailey ran her hands down her long tunic again before opening the door, her heart beating loudly in her ears.

Damn she loved the look of this man.

He wore an old leather jacket that fit firmly to his shoulders and made her want to peel it right off him. His legs were encased in faded denim, but the jeans weren't too old with holes or anything—just perfectly fit to his legs in the ideal blue. The black boots he wore only accentuated the sexy bad-boy image that made her heart beat even faster.

He'd put a knitted beanie on his bald head since it was still a bit cold outside despite the fact that it had warmed up some that day. Of course, with Denver weather, it could drop below freezing tomorrow and then be almost shorts weather the next day.

"Wow," she whispered, and he grinned at her.

"You're pretty wow yourself." He stuck his hands in his pockets and rocked back on his heels. His eyes were bright, as if he wasn't sure how he'd ended up here either. Of course, she was probably just projecting.

"So…you want to come in?" She bit her lip. Why was this so awkward? This was *Sloane*. They saw each other practically every day. He was in her shop more often than not just to talk. Or in Sloane's case, to grunt and mumble unless something was truly important to him. They knew each other…so why did this feel different?

Because it *was* different.

He tilted his head, studying her face. "If that's what you want. I have reservations at Illusion in a bit, but I can move that if you want to do something different." He grinned again. "I didn't actually ask you what you wanted to do after all."

She let out a breath. "We did this a little backward, didn't we?"

He shrugged. "So what? We're doing this, whatever this is, our way. That's all that matters. So, why don't you go put a jacket on and we'll head to Illusion. We'll figure the rest out when we do."

She nodded, oddly warming at his words. She liked the use of the word *our*. She hadn't been an *our* in far too long. As soon as she got her jacket and purse, she locked the door behind her and stood on the front porch with Sloane. He slid his large, calloused hand over hers and she licked her lips.

He'd touched her in the past, of course; slight caresses or a small pat on the back.

But he'd never held her hand.

This was *happening*.

"Ready?" he asked, his voice low, deep.

Was she ready? She wasn't sure she'd ever be ready, but here she was, with Sloane, as whole as she could be and about to take a leap.

"Yeah," she whispered. "Yes, I am," she said a little more clearly.

He met her gaze and gave her a nod. "Good." With that, he led her to his truck, a very sexy extended cab with thick tires for the winter. She knew he also had a bike he used whenever it was warm, and she'd always imagined riding behind him, her thighs wrapped around his body as they rode.

She blushed, annoyed with herself for even blushing in the first place, and pushed those thoughts from her mind.

Date first.

Sex later.

As soon as Sloane got into the cab, he raised a brow at her. "Either you're cold from standing outside too long with me or you're thinking dirty thoughts."

She snorted and waved her hand. "I forget you know me so well."

He licked his lips. "Does that mean you're thinking dirty thoughts?"

This was Sloane, she told herself once more. She could be herself.

"So what if I was? You're sexy, and I was thinking of your bike."

He smiled then, his teeth white against the tan of his skin. "When the weather gets warmer, I'll take you for a ride."

Of course, her mind immediately went to the thought of riding *him*. And then the idea of her riding on his bike in general. Did he mean that he wanted her with him, as in *with* him, on that bike or was it just a friend thing?

And why the hell was she thinking so hard.

"Stop thinking so hard."

She gave him a side-eye as he drove. "Stop reading my mind."

"I can't help it. It's just what we do."

"True," she mumbled. "What *are* we doing, Sloane?" She hadn't meant for that last part to come out, but she apparently couldn't hold it in.

He let out a sigh and gripped the steering wheel a little tighter, as evidenced from the whiteness of his knuckles.

"I'm taking you out. We're going to eat, talk a bit, then we'll figure it out."

She pressed her lips together. "And? And what then? I mean why now? Why did you wait until Brody asked me out to do anything?"

He let out a little growl then pulled over to the side of the road. Her eyes widened as he put on his flashers and turned to her.

"Okay, let's get this straight. You and I? We've been circling each other for a while now. I know it. You know it. So let's just say it."

She nodded. "Yeah, you're right about that, but—"

"I'm not done."

She snorted but waved for him to continue. She kind of liked him all growly and broody—God help her.

"I liked the dance we had even though I hated it. I've wanted you, Hailey, but…well, for reasons of my own, I stayed away. I know I'm not good enough for you, but I don't damn well seem to care right now. I love what we have, love that we talk and I watch you bake, but I want more." He paused for a moment. "I don't know as I deserve it, but I want it. And for the record? You could have asked me out anytime before now. You're not one to back away. You have your secrets, but you say what you want most times."

She swallowed hard, her mind whirling. "I guess I could have asked you out before. And you're right. I *do* have secrets, and that's why I didn't do anything about it."

He studied her face once more. "Well, we're doing something about it now. So let's move on from why we didn't before and figure out what we're going to do next. I know those secrets of ours are going to come out, but—"

This time, she interrupted him. "But if we keep going in circles, we'll only end up hurting each other."

"Exactly. So, does Illusion sound good to you still? Or do you want something different? I know you work with food every day, so you choose."

Illusion was a hipster place that had popped up in downtown Denver a few months ago. It wasn't as pretentious as many of the new hipster places tended to be, and they had fantastic food. They were a hole-in-the-wall that tended to be busy—hence the reservations for dinner. But everything was organic and tasty. Since Hailey only ate organic thanks to the chemicals she'd pumped her body full of in her effort to get healthy, it worked for her.

"Let's go," she said softly and took a breath.

Sloane reached out and cupped her cheek. Without thinking, she leaned into his touch. "Okay, then, Hails. Let's get some food."

He let her go, turned off the hazards, and pulled out onto the road again. All the while, Hailey sat back, her cheek still warm from his touch. She had no idea what she was doing, but damn it, she couldn't wait to figure it out.

"Do you want to come in?" Hailey asked a couple of hours later, her belly full and her cheeks aching from laughing all night.

Dinner with Sloane had been memorable to say the least. He was all big, bearded, broody, and inked. And oh so hers for the evening. He'd laughed with her, touched her when he could—a casual brush of fingers along silk. He would lean in close to tell her a joke and then smile wide when she laughed.

Sloane didn't smile enough.

The fact that he would in her presence warmed her.

Sloane stood next to her on her porch, his large body towering over her but not scaring her in the least. He was the largest man she knew, and yet she knew, without a doubt, he'd never physically hurt her.

"I could get warm," he answered.

She swallowed hard, unlocked her front door and stepped inside, feeling his warm body behind her. He helped her slide off her coat, his fingers brushing along her ribs. She shuddered out a breath.

When he pulled her to face him, she tilted her head up and licked her lips.

"I've wanted to kiss you for a long while," Sloane said softly. "Should have done it before."

"Then do it now," she whispered.

When he lowered his head, pressing his lips to hers, she surrendered to him. She wrapped her arms around his neck and pressed her body to his, aware she was doing something she had not done since the diagnosis

Willingly allowing another to know the feel of her body.

It had taken years for her to allow herself to think of her body as beautiful. As brave. And with this kiss, she would take it one step further.

She would allow another to hopefully think the same.

His tongue slid along hers, and she moaned, loving his taste, the feel of him...everything.

When he pulled away, they were both breathless, a fundamental part of their relationship forever changed.

She met his gaze and knew there was something she had to do before she took the next step. It wouldn't be fair if she didn't.

"I...I've wanted to do that for far too long," she finally said.

Sloane grinned, though she saw an emotion pass through his eyes she couldn't quite name. Secrets, she thought again, they both had secrets. So, perhaps it was time she shared hers. She'd hidden them for so long, she almost didn't know the words.

When she pulled away, he frowned. But he let her go, his fingers lingering on her hips as she moved.

"I'm glad we did it, then. How about we do it again?" he asked.

She licked her lips but held up her hand as he took a step forward. "I need to tell you something first."

He tilted his head. "Okay."

She let out a little laugh. "You're always like that. You say okay and you *listen*. That's what I've always liked about you, Sloane."

He shrugged. "No use in being here if I'm not going to listen. You want to sit down?"

She shook her head. "No, but let's go into the living room anyway. I don't want to be so close to the windows."

His brows raised, but he took her hand and walked with her into the living room. Her heart beat hard and her blood pounded in her ears once more, but this time, it wasn't in breathless anticipation.

"So…you know how we were talking about secrets? Well, I think I should tell you mine…you know…before we do anything else."

He shook his head. "You don't have to tell me anything you're not ready for. I know we started off tonight, hell *today*, on an odd note, but if we're going to do this, let's do it our way. Remember?"

"I want to do this." She closed her eyes. "It's so much harder to date someone you know," she mumbled.

He let out a snort. "The 'get to know you' part is out of the way. You know my favorite drink, and I know the faces you make when you're tired or annoyed. So yeah, we can't hide things like that from each other. But I know you hold something back from everyone, from me. I don't fault you for that. We all need our secrets."

She nodded. "I know. And I should have told everyone long ago. I didn't mean to keep it to myself for so long. It's not that I'm ashamed…" She paused. "I'm not ashamed. But it's…it's not an easy subject. And all of us—the Montgomerys and crew—have been through so much. And since my…thing is in the past, it was hard to bring up."

Sloane took a step forward but didn't touch her. "Tell me, Hailey. You know you can tell me anything. What happened?"

She raised her chin, knowing it was all or nothing. "I had cancer. Breast cancer. In the course of my treatment, I had a bilateral mastectomy. The shape you see now isn't who I was, but it is who I am now. I'm a survivor, Sloane, but no one knows."

Chapter Four

Sloane quit breathing. Just quit breathing, his mind going in a thousand directions yet not moving at all.

"Cancer," he breathed. "Breast cancer."

Jesus. He still couldn't breathe.

"Yep. The big C. I'm cancer free now, by the way. I didn't say that before. I'm actually surprised I said as much as I did. I mean, I practiced saying it in the mirror, but as I haven't told anyone in years, it was hard. Different. You know?"

She kept rambling, and he took two steps toward her, gripped her upper arms, and crushed his mouth to hers. Emotion poured through him and his body shook. She gasped into his mouth before kissing him back.

When he pulled away, he rested his forehead on hers and let out a shuddered breath. "I almost lost you before I met you. I don't know what I'd have done if I'd never had you in my life, Hailey."

Her hands went to his stomach, just resting there. He relaxed at her touch, even as his belly leapt at the feel of her hands on him.

"Sloane."

He moved to cup her face and used his thumb to brush away the single tear that had fallen. "Fuck, Hailey. I knew you were hiding something, but I had no idea it was this. You had *cancer* and didn't tell anybody." He thought about what he knew of her past and frowned. "Wait, how old were you? Did you have anyone?"

She shook her head between his hands, and he let her go but did his best to keep his touch on her.

"I was twenty when I was diagnosed. It took two weeks from the results to my surgery. Since I was Stage 1B, I had a great chance, but they wanted to work fast before it spread to other parts of my body. The tumor was small, thank God, but it was just at the edge of being large enough where they'd been worried. I opted for them to take off both breasts rather than just the right one." Her hand went up to her chest and he looked down, his mind still whirling.

"But you were alone. Weren't you?"

She nodded. "You know my dad left when I was a kid, and my mom died when I was eighteen. I wasn't able to afford college full-time, so I was taking night classes while working at a bakery. I thank that place every day for what they gave me. Not only did they teach me how to do what I love now, but the job gave me benefits so I could afford the treatments."

She continued, and he kept silent, not knowing what to say. What was there to say when the woman he *loved* had almost died and he hadn't known?

"I went through chemo and radiation, but both treatments were relatively short because it hadn't spread. I was lucky. I know that sounds weird to say since it was cancer, but I was lucky."

"Hails."

She gave him a sad smile. "It took six surgeries for them to reconstruct my chest. I'm not the same. Not even a little bit, but I'm me."

He ran a hand down her arm and gripped her hand. She squeezed it. Hard. "You're beautiful, Hailey. Inside and out. I've always known that. But that you have the strength you do, the courage you have after all of that? I am in awe of you."

She pressed her lips together and her eyes filled with tears.

"Shit. I didn't mean to make you cry."

She shook her head and smiled. "It's a good cry. I wasn't sure what you would say. You're a man of few words, after all."

She was not the first person to say that. "I speak when it's important. And you're important."

Far too important for him. Hell, he was dirt, tainted compared to her. And he was so fucking big. He could break her with one careless move. How could he ever think he was good enough for her? At the same time, he knew if he walked away right then, he'd not only regret it forever, but she'd think it was because of her.

She wrung her hands together and bit her lip.

"What is it?"

"I've wanted to tell you for a long while. Not because it was a huge weight on me, even though it was, but more so because…" She let out a breath. "I don't have nipples anymore. I mean, they took them away when they did the first surgery. I will never have the kind of sensation I once had. It's impossible. But I've always wanted to do…something."

He froze. Austin and Maya had done a few nipple tattoos at the shop where they made the ink almost realistic. It was hard, but a tattoo that Sloane knew took courage beyond what others thought. All of those at Montgomery Ink had tattooed over and through scars in their line of work. Hell, it was how Austin had met his wife, Sierra.

But he wasn't sure he could deal with Maya or Austin doing Hailey's ink. He knew he had no right to be possessive, but he wanted to be the one to help her…if that was what she wanted.

"I don't want nipple tattoos. I just don't think they're for me. But I do want something. I've been toying with the idea of art across my chest for a while. I've just needed the courage to tell my story and then do something about it."

He took a deep breath. "I think you have far more courage than you give yourself credit for."

She smiled at him, breaking his heart all over again. "I've always thought…" She stopped, frowned. "I've always thought I should have you do it. I don't know why. I mean, I know we've wanted each other, we've said so tonight. But this is different. I always thought you could help me. But I've been scared."

He leaned forward again and kissed her softly, his heart beating rapidly in his chest. "I would be honored to help you. You can trust me, Hails. I'll take care of you."

She put her hands on his chest and moved forward. "I *do* trust you. That's why I told you. Why I want you to do my ink."

Sloane kissed her again. "I'll do anything you need me to do. And when you're ready for me to start it, I'll be by your side, making sure it's exactly what you need. For you to ask me this…" he shook his head. "You blow me away, Hailey. You fucking blow me away."

She smiled at him then, and he was lost.

He loved this woman, loved everything about her, and now he had fallen that much deeper. He just prayed he could keep her.

The bomb blast hit his Humvee hard, and his brain rattled. Sloane gasped for breath, the fire burning around him all but searing his skin. He reached for his brother, but couldn't feel him. Couldn't feel much of anything.

Just the pain.

Sloane sat up in bed, sweat pouring from his skin as he tried to swallow. Only he couldn't breathe, and he had to keep his heart from pounding right out of his chest.

Fuck.

He hadn't had one of those nightmares in years. He knew he'd never rightly forget that day, but he thought he'd move past the night terrors that kept him up, that kept his hands unsteady and his eyes red-rimmed.

Sloane grunted as he pulled his legs to the side of the bed and rested his head in his hands. He just needed to take a few deep breaths and then he'd be fine. He'd done this countless times before. PTSD didn't go away with happy thoughts and willpower alone. He knew it might never go away, but at least he wasn't struggling on a day-to-day basis. He was doing far better than some of his friends from the service. Hell, at least he'd come home whole. Or even come home at all. His body might be covered in scars, but he'd kept his limbs and his sight.

That had to count for something.

The thought of loss and coming through made him think of Hailey and he sobered rapidly. He'd only been to war. Only fought and lived, coming out mostly whole.

She'd lost far more than he had.

And yet he felt like she was doing so much better than him. She'd fought with grace, or at least he figured she had. She'd even told him about the tattoo she wanted *him* to give her. When he thought of his situation, all he'd done was live—when so many hadn't.

No one else in that truck had lived through that roadside bomb.

Only him.

How was it *he* deserved to be here? How did he deserve to come home and be with a woman who made him feel like everything would be okay?

He didn't deserve it.

But he was just selfish enough to go through with it. Somehow, he'd have to figure out how to live with that.

After he'd kissed her again the night before, he'd told himself he needed to leave. There had been a lot said that day, and they both needed time to let it all sink in before they took the next step. As they'd both said the night before, they were past some of the initial awkwardness that came with getting to know someone on a date. They were already friends, already close. Now they would be closer. He didn't know when they would sleep together, but he knew it would happen once she was ready.

He frowned. She'd said she had no nipple sensation, but did she lose anything else?

Sloane would have to ask her that outright. There was no way he'd hurt her if he had the chance to make things easier for her in the long run. Maybe he'd do some research on what others dealt with so he knew the right questions to ask. Considering he knew from his own therapy with PTSD that everyone's treatments and aftermaths were unique, Hailey wouldn't be textbook. But at least he'd be somewhat prepared when and if they went to bed together.

They weren't young, well, he wasn't anyway, so he wasn't going to be some nervous kid when it came to sex. He'd make sure she got what she needed and do his best not to screw it up by hurting her in some way. It wasn't that she was different from other women he'd been with—though she was because she was *Hailey*—it was just that he was so fucking scared. He wanted to make sure he didn't mess up.

Somehow, in the course of a day, he'd gone from standing to the side, being near her but not with her, to dating her. He didn't know if they had a label, but it was at least a new step in a direction he wasn't sure he'd ever be ready for.

Sloane stood up and ran a hand over his head, noting he'd need to shave again soon. He liked the feel of the air on his bald head, so he kept it shaved. He'd done it in basic training and hadn't stopped since. It didn't seem to bother Hailey, so he'd keep it.

Today, he had to go to work and act like nothing happened in front of the others. Sure, they'd heard her storm into his section, but they'd at least pretended not to listen. He didn't want them to give Hailey or him shit. All the while, he'd want to ask her what was going on and scream that he'd kissed her at the top of his lungs.

If he weren't sure of his age, and the fact that he was nearing forty, he would have thought he was some damn teenage boy getting to kiss his first crush.

Hailey was his first for a lot of things, though, so maybe that made sense.

His first friend he'd fallen for. The first woman that he knew would be nothing but serious after getting out of the service.

His first…just his first chance at Hailey.

By the time he made it to Montgomery Ink, his head ached from too many thoughts and lack of coffee. He hadn't made any at home, and he wasn't sure if he should go into Taboo and get some from Hailey. Seriously, it was like he was a teenager again.

When he had the time, he should just go over there for coffee and see her.

Things had changed, but *they* hadn't. And once he remembered that, everything would be okay. At least he hoped so.

Sloane stretched his back as he took a seat at his station. He had three appointments that day—two smaller ones that he could get done in less than an hour each—and another one that would take most of the afternoon. That one he knew had to be perfect. Not that any of his work was less than perfect, but the one that afternoon had to be better than the rest.

While each of the artists at Montgomery Ink did all kinds of work, they each had some specialties they were known for. Sloane had become known for his remembrance pieces. Those who had lost someone in the service came to him. He'd done ink remembering fallen soldiers—men, women, and dogs—as well as those who wanted to remember their branch in general.

Today he was doing an eagle for someone and wanted to make sure he got the feathers just right. The bird would look as if it were taking off; its wings stretched back, legs bent.

He hated and loved doing these all at the same time.

Maybe, just maybe, if he could help others, he'd rid himself of the stain of blood on his hands. Only he knew that wasn't an option. He'd be tainted until the day he died—and he refused to let that time be short. The men who had fallen by his side deserved far more than what they'd received, and Sloane refused to give up when they hadn't had a chance.

He let out a shuddering breath, pushing the memories back. It usually wasn't this bad, but for some reason, he couldn't quite get out of this funk.

Of course, he knew the reason, and she was just a wall away, working and probably smiling. Giving in to temptation had done something to him, broken down the barriers that had held the panic at bay.

"So...what happened last night?" Maya asked. He lifted his head to see her leaning against the table in his station, her pierced brow raised.

He leaned back and folded his arms over his chest. Rather than answer, he just stared at her.

She narrowed her eyes. "You're not going to answer me, are you?"

He remained silent.

She threw up her hands. "Fine. But if you hurt her, I'll kick your ass. Oh, and if she hurts you, I'll kick her ass. I'm an equal opportunity ass kicker."

Sloane smiled then. "I've always admired that about you."

Maya flipped him off then went back to her station, leaving Sloane alone with his thoughts. When he had the time, he should just go over there for coffee and see her. He didn't like not knowing what to say—hence why most people thought he was the silent type. He only spoke when it was important and he knew the words. *This* was important. But he didn't know the words.

So, instead of going next door and seeing her like he wanted to, he stayed put and waited for his first client. He'd go over there eventually. He couldn't hide from her.

And that's what scared him.

The day thankfully passed quickly, and he stood up, rolling his neck to try and get the crick out. His stomach grumbled and he cursed himself. Somehow, he'd gone through most of the day without eating anything except the protein bar he'd found in his desk. Who knew how old that thing was. In the past, Callie might have gone and gotten the crew lunch, but now that she was a full-time artist and not an apprentice, she was just far too busy. Autumn, Griffin Montgomery's woman, worked up front most days, but today had been her day off. That meant he'd been forced to get his own food and hadn't had the time between clients.

"Go get food or go home," Austin said from his station.

Sloane looked over at his friend. "What?"

"You haven't eaten today, and that's fucking stupid in our line of work. You don't have any clients on the docket and the walk-ins aren't that bad today. Maya, Callie, and I can handle the influx."

Sloane ran a hand down the back of his neck. "We need more artists."

Austin nodded. "I'm putting out my feelers for someone who can be here for as many hours as we are. Or maybe I can get another apprentice."

There were four other artists that worked there on partial shifts, but they weren't full time since they either lived too far away or had other jobs. What they needed was another full timer.

"If I hear anything, I'll let you know," Sloane added.

"Good. Now go next door, see your woman, and get some food. Head home and take her with you. Or at least make her go home. She's been here as long as you have I bet."

His woman.

He sure loved the sound of that. But was it the truth? Was she his? They hadn't truly discussed what they were doing, other than that they were taking it one moment at a time. The fact she'd bared her secrets to him had meant more than anything.

Sloane nodded at his boss, then the others, before cleaning up his station. After, he headed into Taboo through the side door and stopped two feet in.

She was magnificent.

Her teeth bit into her lip as she fought not to laugh at whatever Sierra, Austin's wife, had said. She had flour on her apron, but other than that, she looked pristine—not like a woman who had probably been on her feet for a full shift.

He'd always known she was strong, but now that he knew the truth, he saw the depth of that strength. He was a big man—big hands, large chest—just *big*. He could break her if he weren't careful.

He could break her with more than his strength, he knew. The fragility that slid under the surface of her skin wasn't easy to see, but he saw it. She could be the strongest woman in the world and still carry that.

He couldn't hurt her.

But he just might.

She turned to him then and smiled, though there was wariness in her eyes. It made sense, after all. He hadn't come by for coffee and this was the first time they'd seen each other since he'd left her house the night before. He wasn't sure if he should go to her, kiss her senseless, then carry her out of the building over his shoulder, or stay here and watch her from afar.

He stuck his hands in his pockets and let his smile rise just a little so she would know he liked seeing her.

Sierra looked between them and smiled like the Grinch at Christmas. She all but rubbed her hands together in glee. Of course, he only saw this out of the corner of his eye, as the rest of his attention was on the blonde in front of him—the blonde he wanted in his arms.

"Hey," he said.

"Hey."

Sierra clapped her hands together, this time in truth, and slid off her stool. "Hi, Sloane. I'm going to head to Harry and Marie's to pick up the kids." She grinned. "They wanted time with the grandbabies today. Hailey was just telling me she was done for the day since her closing crew is here. Perfect timing."

She waved and said her good-byes before she headed through the door to Montgomery Ink, presumably to kiss her husband on her way out.

That left Sloane and Hailey awkwardly standing in front of one another in silence.

Hailey cleared her throat. "Uh, yeah, I was about to get off."

He wanted to get her off.

Jesus, his mind needed to stay out of the gutter.

From the way her cheeks blushed, her mind had gone there, too. Interesting.

"Want to get something to eat?" he asked. His stomach rumbled then. Loudly. He winced. "Apparently, I really need to eat."

She smiled then and waved at the counter. "Let me get you some stew. It's the kind you like. I'll get a bowl, too."

He met her gaze. "Can we take it to go?"

She studied his face for a moment then nodded. "That I can do. Where are we going?" She bit her lip again, this time her gaze traveling down his body, slowly.

"Your place," he whispered, and she sucked in a shaky breath.

"Oh. Okay." She looked up again and licked her lips. "We can do that." She turned back to the kitchen, and he swallowed hard.

He didn't know what they would do once they got there, but he couldn't wait to find out. She came back quickly, her jacket on and a large bag in her hands. He took it from her, their hands brushing.

They both sucked in a breath, and he had to smile. "I'll follow you," he said softly before leaning down to brush a kiss against her lips.

She pressed closer and he had to hold back a groan. They were in public—her shop and place of business. It wouldn't do to have him pick her up by the waist and place her on the counter so he could get a better angle at her mouth.

He'd have to wait for them to be alone for that.

When he pulled back, she licked her lips again. "See you at my place," she breathed, then took his hand and led them to the parking lot.

The relief that hit him was heady. He'd been afraid they'd have to hide this since things were so new, but that wasn't the case. He hadn't thought twice about leaning down to kiss her once he'd seen her, and he was damn lucky she hadn't pulled back too quickly.

They needed to talk, but first…first he needed her taste.

As soon as they entered her home, she locked the door behind them and pressed her back against the hard wood.

"Hungry?" she asked.

He nodded but set the bag down on the entry table. "Yeah, I am. But I think food can wait."

She smiled then. "Good."

He cupped her face then crushed his mouth to hers. Her lips parted for him, and he tangled his tongue with hers, both of their resounding moans going straight to his dick. She put both hands on his back, her fingernails digging into his beat-up leather jacket.

That wouldn't do.

He wanted to *feel*. He pulled away then tugged off his jacket and threw it on the floor before doing the same to hers.

"You want this, Hails?" he asked, his voice ragged. He needed to know before he moved on.

She reached up and bit his chin, sending a shock down his back. "Yes. I want you. I've wanted you for years. I wanted you to come over today and kiss me good morning, but I'm glad you didn't. Because if you had, then I'd have taken you to my office and had you right there on my desk. Probably not the best way to try and get work done."

He stared at her a moment, then threw his head back and laughed. "Jesus, I'm so fucking glad I'm not alone. I tried to keep you off my mind like I have for so long, but it didn't work. When I wasn't thinking about if I should come over to your side or not, I was thinking about what I wanted to do to you as soon as I saw you. It's bad, Hails. I want you so much that I don't know if I can be gentle."

"Sloane…"

He ran his hands up her rib cage and stopped right under her breasts. "You need to tell me what to do, Hails. I don't want to hurt you."

"You can't hurt me," she whispered, though they both knew that wasn't quite the truth. But they didn't talk about that. Couldn't talk about that.

When he moved to cup her breast, she sucked in a breath. "Tell me what to do." She didn't feel any different than what he'd thought she'd feel like, but damn if he'd hurt her.

"You're doing it. I'm not made of glass, Sloane."

He leaned down and pressed his mouth to her temple. "You're far stronger than glass, but I want to make this good for you."

"I'm pretty sure it's impossible for you not to."

He kissed down her neck, and she tilted her head to give him better access. "I'm not going to make love to you for the first time against a door. The first time we'll be in your bed." He kissed her again. "Next time we can be against the door. Or on the table. Or in the shower."

She let out a shuddering breath. "I take it you have this all planned out."

"Not quite that, but I've thought about all of it."

She tilted her head up to meet his gaze. "Me, too."

He pressed his mouth to hers and pulled his hand away from her breast. As she wrapped her arms around his neck, he reached around to cup her ass in his hands and lifted her off the ground. She let out a little squeak along his mouth, and he kissed her harder. When he moved toward her bedroom, she wrapped her legs around his waist, her heat pressed hard against him.

Fuck. He wasn't going to last long.

As soon as he got to her bedroom, he set her down and pulled away so he could study her face.

She bit her lip then tugged on the bottom of her shirt. "I...I've only been with one other person since the surgeries. I know you don't want to hear about other men, but I wanted to make sure you know that you won't be the first to see my scars other than my doctor." She pressed her lips together. "You'll be the second, actually."

He ground his teeth together at the thought of her with another man but pushed it away as fast as he could. She was telling him this for a reason and he got it, but it didn't mean he had to like it. From the hesitant way she moved, he had a feeling the asshole before him hadn't done his job. Sloane would be damned if he'd allow that to happen again.

"Like I said, tell me what to do."

"Just make love to me," she whispered. With that, she pulled her shirt over her head and let out a breath. He could see the scars on her stomach, the port scars on her chest. The bra she wore covered most of her, but he could tell she'd had surgery.

He moved closer then put one hand around her back to the clasp of her bra. He leaned down and kissed her softly. When he undid the clasp, she moved her arms so the bra fell on the floor between them, tangling with their feet.

"It's not pretty," she said, her voice stronger than before. "But it took me a long time to realize I'm beautiful despite the scars."

Sloane pulled away and looked into her eyes before dropping his gaze to her chest. His heart constricted at the sight of what had almost taken her from him.

"You're beautiful *with* the scars, Hailey." And that was true. Her surgeon had done a fantastic job, but even if they hadn't been as precise as they obviously were, she'd have been beautiful.

Long scars bisected each breast and smaller ones marred the undersides. Parts of her skin had dimpled or scrunched together as the tissue and muscles underneath had been moved around during her healing.

"I don't look like I once did."

He tilted his head at her and nodded. "No one does. You look like a fucking survivor, Hailey. That's all that matters to me. You get that? You're *here*. You're here to be with me and that's what I know. You're alive, breathing, fucking *thriving*. What more can I ask for? So you don't have nipples? So what? You're *here*."

Tears filled her eyes and she reached up to wipe them away. He took her hand quickly before wiping her tears away himself.

"I'm not going to lie to you, Hailey. I won't do that. I know you don't look like you once did, but fuck, I don't either." He pulled back and took off his shirt. Scars covered his back and sides, as well as most of his chest. Surgical scars, scars from cuts and abrasions, as well as a few burn scars dotted his skin.

"Oh, Sloane…" She reached out and brushed her fingers along the largest one—a mix of burn and jagged lines. "I didn't know."

He shrugged but put his hand over hers before pulling her palm so it rested over his heart. "I hid them like you hid yours. No reason for others to know and not know what to say, to feel. But you're not anyone. You're Hailey. We're both scarred, but we're *here*."

And those he'd left behind weren't.

But he wouldn't think about that now.

Not when he had Hailey in front of him, bared in body and soul.

"Will you tell me about them?" she asked.

At first he thought she was talking about the men he'd lost, but then he knew she was speaking of the scars. Of course, they went together in a way, and he knew he'd have to tell her everything eventually.

"Not right now. Let me love you first."

"Okay," she said. "I'll hold you to that."

"Just let me hold you."

Sloane kissed her again, running his lips along her neck before kneeling in front of her. Hailey's body shook, but she placed her hands on his shoulders. When he kissed her left breast and the scar that resided there, he felt the first tear drop on his head. He kept going, kissing each scar, each mark that had cost her, but in the end, had saved her. Without the pain, without the scars, he would have lost her before he'd had her. And he'd never forget that.

While Hailey might not be able to feel his touch here the same way she once might have, he wanted to love her in every way he could. They both would come tonight, would make love until they were spent, but first, he needed to love her body.

All of her body.

He might be too large, too jagged, too haunted, but he'd make this special for her.

He couldn't suck on her, play with her the way he might have with another woman, but there were still things he could do. By the time he moved his lips across her chest, and then down her belly, she had her hands on his head, pressing him closer.

He pulled back and grinned. "Bet you wish I had hair for you to pull right about now."

She sniffed, though her eyes were dark with desire. "I…I *felt* that, Sloane. It wasn't…it wasn't like before, but you kissing me…"

He quickly moved to his feet and crushed his mouth to hers. She gasped and pressed her body to his. His hard cock rocked against her belly and he groaned.

When he pulled away, he moved them both to the bed then pulled her pants down in a quick move. She gasped and laughed when they caught on her shoes.

He snorted, then undid her shoes and threw her pants across the room. "Next time we take our shoes off at the door."

She met his gaze. "Deal."

He quickly pulled off his clothes—shoes first—and climbed into bed with her. They kissed again, their hands roaming over each other's bodies until they were both left breathless. When she went to grip his cock, he stilled her.

"If you touch me right now, I'll come and ruin the rest of our night." He groaned when she slid her foot up his calf. "I'm not as young as I once was."

"I forgot I'm dating such an older man."

He let her go, only to reach around and smack her ass. "Sassy."

"You know it."

Sloane licked his lips then cursed before getting up and searching for his wallet and the condom he'd left in there.

"That thing still good?" she asked.

"Yep," he said and came back to her while rolling the condom on his length. "I put it there this morning."

"Feeling cocky?" she teased.

He covered her body before he pressed the tip of his cock to her entrance. "You're about to feel my cock."

She groaned. "Bad joke, Sloane."

"True, but you'll still feel it. All of it." With that, he kissed her again, thrusting his hips and filling her in one move. They both groaned, their bodies shaking.

"You're...bigger than I thought."

He couldn't help but grin. "Thank you." He kissed her. "And you're fucking tight as hell."

"Thank you," she teased then gasped as he moved.

He tangled their fingers together and kept his gaze on hers. Her eyes darkened and her mouth parted as they made love, slowly, eternally. They'd be different another time, be harder, hotter, or whatever they needed. But for now, for that moment, they were *them*.

He wasn't a poet, wasn't someone in touch with his feelings, but with Hailey under him, her trust and body in his arms—literally—he felt like he could die right then and find heaven.

Though he didn't want to leave her, didn't want to lose her.

As he thrust once more, her pussy clenching around him like a vise, he came with her, their hearts beating as one, their breaths coming in pants.

She was his, if only for the moment.

And if he tried hard enough, he might not fuck it up. But he knew himself, knew his past.

He wanted her, wanted *this* until the end of his days, but he was Sloane Gordon, and he didn't get happy endings.

He never had...and he never would.

Chapter Five

Hailey was sore in all the best places and out of her damn mind. She and Sloane had made love two more times the night before—despite Sloane saying he wasn't a young man anymore. He might be a full decade older than her, but there was nothing old about those moves of his.

While she'd always known they'd be explosive in bed—there was no way a man built like Sloane, a man so good with his hands, would be anything but amazing—she hadn't known it would be *that*...hot.

He'd been so slow and careful at first—each kiss, each breath pleasure-filled and achingly tender. And as they explored one another, their heat ramped up and turned...molten.

Her heart hurt at the thought of how sweet and sexy he'd been.

And now she had no idea what the hell she was going to do.

They hadn't talked about what this meant, what their future would hold because that would be too important. They were taking things slow. Well, as slow as they could since they'd already slept together. But she had to remember, they'd been dancing around one another for years.

Falling into bed with one another was inevitable.

Falling in love with him was as well.

If only she knew if he could fall for her.

It hadn't escaped her notice that while she'd told him her secrets, he hadn't done the same for her. She had a feeling it had to do with the scars that marred his body—the depravity of which surprised her. He'd been hurt. Badly. And she hadn't known the depth of that pain. She wanted to, and she prayed that he would tell her what had happened.

But that wouldn't happen unless and until he was ready.

Just because she'd been ready to finally tell him of her past didn't mean he was ready as well. It wasn't fair of her to put her own timeline on his needs. If they kept going as they were, sure and steady, hopefully he'd feel ready to reveal.

Hopefully, he'd open up more and more and be the man she knew he could be beneath the gruff edges.

Still, she didn't know if they had a true future because they hadn't *talked* about it. And that annoyed her to no end. She was a pile of nerves, so unlike herself, that she wasn't sure what the heck she was doing.

"Okay, girl, if you're going to stand in the corner looking like a lost puppy, I'm going to have to kick your ass," Maya said with a grin.

Hailey snorted, then shook out her arms. "Sorry, doll, I'm a little off tonight."

"No shit," Maya said simply and held out a margarita glass filled to the brim. "You're driving so you get a virgin one. In fact, I *only* made virgin frozen strawberry margaritas tonight. Boy, how things have changed."

Sierra rolled her eyes as she drank her frilly, pink, non-alcoholic drink. "We all need to go home and get ready for work tomorrow and spend time with our families. Or we have a thousand other things to do."

Hailey took her drink and went to sit next to Miranda.

"Pretty much," Miranda added. "Decker and I may not have kids, but I still like to see him nightly."

"And you like practicing making those kids," Callie teased.

"I don't need to think about Miranda practicing making babies," Meghan said with a smile. "Though Luc and I *are* practicing as much as we can."

"Bitches," Maya mumbled.

"You're just jealous we're getting laid," Autumn said with a sweet smile.

Maya threw a pillow at her, barely missing Autumn's drink.

"Watch it, doll, you're about to stain your couch," Hailey said.

"I hate you, too," Maya said with narrowed eyes. "I know that blush on your cheeks and the swagger in Sloane's walk. You got laid. It's about time."

Hailey raised her chin. "Yes, I did. There's no point in hiding it. I had hot, dirty, sweaty sex, and I plan to have it again." That much about her relationship she knew.

The girls squealed and did little booty shakes in their chairs.

"All hail Hailey and Sloane!" Maya called out. "To their glorious sex, even though I'm not having any."

"Whoo!" the others chimed in.

Hailey rolled her eyes but took a sip of her drink, wishing it had alcohol in it. "You know, Maya, you could be getting laid. Just saying."

Maya gave her a smile that didn't quite reach her eyes and Hailey wanted to curse. She did her best not to look at the woman currently sitting next to Maya.

Holly was Jake's girlfriend. Serious girlfriend it seemed. Maya and Jake were best friends, though the whole world thought they were something more. Apparently, everybody was wrong, and Maya was doing her best to bring Holly into the fold. Only, sweet and adorable Holly didn't quite fit in—not that they'd let her feel like that. The Montgomerys and crew weren't assholes.

Though Hailey wanted to know more about what was going on in that corner, she knew she had to think about something else. She'd asked the girls—Sierra, Callie, Maya, Holly, Miranda, Meghan, Autumn, and Tabby—to meet up so she could tell them what she should have told them long ago. Autumn was new to her circle, as she'd just recently found love with Griffin Montgomery, and Holly had sort of just shown up since she'd been hanging out with Maya at the time, but Hailey didn't mind that they were there. They'd all gathered at Maya's since that was where they usually met—there or at Taboo. Maya didn't have children, and she had a large living room with tons of space to sit. Plus, she had a kick-ass blender.

"Okay, now that we've made Maya feel bad about the sad state of her sex life, why don't you tell us why you wanted us to meet?" Callie asked.

Hailey let out a breath. "It's like you read my mind. I already told Sloane this, but I wanted to tell you as well. All of you. It's something I should have told you way before this."

Miranda leaned close. "What is it?"

"Seven years ago I was diagnosed with breast cancer." She told them the story as she'd told Sloane, straight and to the point. Yet this time it didn't seem as hard, as if once she'd said it aloud it became easier.

The others cried and moved to hold her close. She let the tears fall as well, the women in this room her family by choice, not by blood. She'd lost everyone else close to her, but at least she had these women—and the men who loved them.

She had Sloane as well, and she had to remember that. As long as they didn't mess up the friendship they had, she could do this. She *could*.

When Meghan cupped her face and kissed her cheek, it brought Hailey out of her thoughts of Sloane and into the present.

"Why didn't you tell us before?" the other woman asked. "Why did you carry this burden yourself?"

Hailey pressed her lips together. "I don't know. At first I was getting to know all of you, and then it was hard to bring up. But I didn't want to hide it anymore." She blew out a breath when Meghan stepped away. "But since I'm talking about it, do your self-exams, ladies. It saved my life. If you feel a lump, you get it biopsied. You do something. Your doctors might not know everything right away, so you ask the hard questions. Get me?"

The others nodded then did a group hug that brought Hailey

peace.

"I love you ladies. Just saying." Hailey hiccupped a laugh then stood back to wipe her tears. "And on that note, I think I'm going to go home and take a long, hot bath. I really just wanted you all in one place to tell you. I know you all have families and work to go home to. But, yeah…"

She said her good-byes as the group broke up and wiped their tears. It had been harder, a hell of a lot harder, to tell Sloane, but she was glad she'd told the others. They would tell their men, tell the Montgomerys, and then she wouldn't have those secrets anymore.

She was free.

Free to go home alone and figure out what the hell she was going to do with Sloane. Ten minutes later, she stepped inside her house and stood in her living room, a little too lost for comfort. What if she messed everything up? What if he did? Why was she so scared of what could happen with him. He liked her for *her*, but what if they made a mistake. What if this ruined what she had with him before…with the Montgomerys. What if…

She cursed at herself.

She was putting herself in a corner when she didn't need to be. This was so unlike her that she hated it.

The knock on her door surprised her, and she looked through the peephole. As soon as she saw Sloane's large form she relaxed, even as her body warmed at the thought of him.

"Hey," she said once she'd opened the door.

He had a six-pack of beer in one hand, a pizza in the other, and a smile on his face. "I heard your girls' night ended early. What do you say about a movie?"

She stepped back and ran her hand down the hardness of his stomach as he passed. "Okay," she said simply.

Okay. They would be okay. If she didn't think so hard, they would be okay.

They had to be.

* * * *

The heat from the bomb flayed his skin and he screamed. He couldn't move, couldn't breathe. The weight of part of the Humvee pushed at his chest and he placed his hands on the edges, growling as it burned his flesh.

He turned to the side, his body going still at the sight of what shouldn't have been.

The five other men at his side stared at him with dead eyes, their mouths hanging open, their jaws unhinging as they screamed a soundless scream. They reached for him, clawing at his body as he tried to break free.

But he could never be free.

The chains of memory, of guilt for living and finding the happiness he was never supposed to find, tightened around his chest, his neck, his gut. He started to suffocate. The five bodies shifted back to their whole forms, young men with no hope in their gazes, only death. They'd been too young to drink but old enough to die in his arms.

Sloane woke up again, his body shaking.

Thank God he'd slept at his own home that night. He'd yet to sleep at Hailey's even though they'd been together more than a few nights already. He knew his dreams well enough that he couldn't predict when they appeared. He didn't want Hailey to have to experience them, or rather him when he had them. And God forbid if he ever woke up swinging, he wouldn't be able to deal with the consequences.

It'd been a couple of years since he'd talked to a professional, but it might be time to do that again. He wasn't afraid of shrinks, but sometimes the ones who hadn't been over there just didn't get it. They said the right things, nodded at the appropriate times, but until they saw their friends dying or a little kid being shot in the head because he'd crossed the street at the wrong time, they just didn't know.

He was fine most days. In fact, he was much better than he used to be. He could sit in busy rooms, deal with loud noises. His symptoms came later, in dreams. He didn't have it as bad as other guys, but he knew the nightmares and the fact that sometimes he broke out into a cold sweat, even during the day, may not ever go away. He'd never been violent, other than needing to box for stress relief sometimes, but he was like that before he'd seen what he'd seen, done what he'd done. Before he'd had Hailey and had opened up a part of himself he wasn't ready to face—let alone let Hailey see.

He didn't usually wake up swinging, but it could happen if he weren't careful. Things weren't rainbows and unicorns. Things didn't just get better. And even if he had the ability to self-reflect and knew he was in pain and knew he had to move on, it wasn't going to happen overnight. It might not ever happen.

And that was something he had to live with.

But it wasn't something he had to force on the woman he loved.

He had brothers who had gone through worse. He knew others had gone through hell. PTSD wasn't something someone could wear a ribbon for and call themselves a fucking ally. It was something that afflicted way too many people, and yet others who didn't understand said to just get over it.

He wouldn't get over it.

And hell, if he got over it, what would happen then? Would he forget his brothers? Forget the ones he'd lost?

He growled to himself, frustrated with the path his thoughts had taken.

Fuck this.

He pulled himself out of bed and made his way to the shower. He pulled the lever to as hot as he could take it, and let it steam up the room when he took care of his business and brushed his teeth. Then he stomped into the stall and tried to wash away the guilt and sin covering him.

If only he had Hailey with him. She'd help. Whenever he was deep inside her, he forgot the pain and only thought of her. At the thought of her, his dick filled and throbbed. He fisted it, his mind going in a thousand different directions, but Hailey was at the forefront. He thought of her warm heat, the way she gasped as she came, the way she raked her nails down his back. He placed one hand on the shower wall and pumped into his hand, squeezing at the base and twisting up in rapid motions.

As he pictured her arching her back, her fingers in her pussy as she looked at him, he came.

Hard.

Spurts of come hit the shower wall then slid down in the now cooling water.

He took a shaky step back then roared. He punched the damn wall, his fist sliding through the poorly made tiles. Pain ricocheted up his arm, and he wasn't sure if he'd broken his hand or not, but he didn't care. He didn't care about anything. He was dirty, stained. Scarred in more ways than one. He'd just fucked his hand, thinking of a woman far too good for him.

He wasn't worth anything. Just a man who should have died with his men instead of living to see another day…living to love her.

It wasn't fair to those who had been lost.

It wasn't fair to her.

As he pulled his hand out of the tile, he winced. Blood dripped down his skin and to the drain below. He flexed his hand, but he didn't feel any burning pain so he figured he'd been fucking lucky. He was a tattoo artist, damn it. He worked with his hands daily, and he could have easily just ruined *everything* in a blind rage.

And what would happen if he ruined it again with Hailey, huh?

He should break it off before they got too close. If he broke it off sooner rather than later, there might still be pieces to pick up so they could keep some semblance of friendship.

But first, he'd help her with her ink. He'd do it because he was an asshole and selfish enough to want it to be *him* to mark her body…even though he couldn't mark her soul.

Not in the way they both needed.

He wasn't good enough for that. And once Hailey realized that, it would all be lost.

And Sloane would be alone.

Where he deserved.

Again.

Chapter Six

There was something wrong with Sloane, but Hailey couldn't figure it out. She ran her hands over her pants, keeping her eyes on him as he stared at his sketchbooks. He might have said all the right things, done the right ones, too, but there was something off with his eyes—as if he truly didn't believe what he was saying.

Or maybe she was just thinking too hard. She did that all the time.

But there was a tension in his shoulders that hadn't been there before.

There was a gruffness to his voice that scared her.

Not in a way that meant pain, but in a way that meant…brokenness. She'd never heard it before, not even in the days when he'd lock himself in the Montgomery Ink office and focus on his sketches rather than the world. He'd do that for hours at a time when he didn't have clients, then come over to Taboo with a need for coffee and food. She'd take care of him and make sure he had enough in him to make it home, but even then, the darkness in his eyes hadn't been like it was now.

She didn't understand it.

It couldn't have been something she did, because, damn it, she hadn't done anything. And she wasn't the type of person to immediately blame herself for every little thing. But he was scaring her enough that she began to wonder if maybe she *had* done something.

And that worried her.

"There a reason you're standing next to me hovering like you want something?" Sloane asked, though there was a smile in his voice. Perhaps not as bright as it had been only days before, but it was something. He set down his pencil and turned to her. He held open his arms, and she slid into them, wrapping her own around his neck.

"I didn't know what to do with my hands," she answered. Her gaze met his and she did her best to try and figure out what was wrong, but that wouldn't happen until she asked him.

And knowing Sloane, he wouldn't tell her.

Sloane's mouth quirked into a grin and he lowered his hands to cup her ass. "I know what I can do with *my* hands, Hails. Why don't you explore with your own and figure out what you need to do with them."

She rolled her eyes but kissed him anyway, a soft kiss that turned into something much hotter, much deeper. Sloane's hand molded her butt, bringing her even closer as they kissed. When she broke away, she had to catch her breath. Then she wiped the lipstick off his lips.

"Sorry about that," she said when she showed him her thumb.

He shrugged and kissed her thumb anyway. "I think it makes my lips pop, don't you?"

She threw back her head and laughed, aware his hands were still on her ass. "It accentuates your skin tone for sure. But really, sorry it's all over your lips. I didn't wear the stain today since I like to try different things, but I guess I'm not used to having to worry about rubbing it off on another person's body."

He licked his lips, his eyes on her own. "Oh, really...what part of my body are you thinking of putting your lips on?"

She lowered her head so she could run her teeth along his earlobe. When he shuddered against her, she bit down slightly. "Where do you want my lips?"

His grip on her tightened, and she let out a happy sigh.

"Anywhere you want them, Hails. Anywhere you want them." He squeezed her again but didn't move her closer. "Before we get naked and show each other exactly where we want to put our lips, though, I want to work on your ink. I have a few ideas sketched, but I can't do much more without your input and without tracing your outline."

She gulped but nodded. Her body cooled somewhat—not that it ever completely cooled in Sloane's presence. They were in his home office because he'd wanted to do the outlining in private. Eventually, when he did the actual ink, he'd close off part of the shop so it would just be the two of them and no one would see if she didn't want them to. While that was standard practice for intimate tattoos, she still loved the fact that he took care of her.

She also hadn't been to Sloane's that often, so it was nice to see where he lived, be among his things. It wasn't a large place, and frankly a little stark, but it smelled of him. And except for the construction work in the bathroom where it looked like he was redoing tiles, everything seemed to be in order.

And if she thought about tiling a bathroom, she wouldn't have to think about the fact that they were about to outline her chest so she could get the tattoo she'd wanted for years.

Sloane moved his hands to cup her face. "Hails."

She blinked at him.

"We don't have to do this now. We don't have to do this ever. The ink you get is for *you*. Yeah, I might see it when your shirt is off, but anything we do from here on out is for you."

The way he said that made her pause. *Might?* Did that mean he might *not* see her once it was done?

She forced those thoughts from her head and focused on him. "I want to. It's just a lot. You know?"

He brushed her cheek with his thumb. "I know. And we don't have to do anything today. We can just make out."

She winked, some of the tension going out of her shoulders. "Can we make out after?"

"It's a deal." He kissed her softly then turned her around so she sat in his lap. She could feel his erection under her, but neither of them said anything about it. Not yet.

"So you already did some sketches?" she asked. She didn't reach out and trace the leather-bound book in front of her, but she wanted to. This was *his,* so she would restrain herself.

He fisted his hand in her hair and she melted on his lap. When he pushed her hair to the side and kissed behind her ear, she melted more, causing both of them to moan.

"Hails, baby, don't squirm or I'm going to fuck you right here and we're never going to get your ink done."

"You're the one fisting my hair and kissing my neck."

He pulled on her hair, and she moaned.

She didn't move, but she *did* bite into her lip. "So." She cleared her throat. "Sketches."

He let her hair down and kissed her temple. "I didn't know what you wanted since we hadn't gotten that far. I don't know if you want flowers or symbols or anything. But I was up late and had an idea. You don't have to use this. In fact, I suggest you don't. And though I know your body quite well now that my hands and mouth have been on every inch of you, I don't know it to the detail I'd need for a tattoo. So things would have to change anyway depending on angles and shit. But, if you like it as a base, then sure. I just couldn't get it out of my head. You know?"

"I know." She leaned into him. The fact that he'd thought of something for her, as if he couldn't *stop* from sketching it, brought a warmth to her chest she didn't want to think about just then. "Show me."

Sloane reached around her and opened the book, his hands steady, but she could feel the tension in his body. This was important to him. Not just the ink he would eventually place on her skin, but what he was going to show her. It was important to her, as well.

She sucked in a breath at the first drawing. "Sloane."

He didn't say anything, but she let her shaky hand reach out and trace the edge of the paper. "How...how did you know?"

"What do you mean?"

"It's…it's almost exactly what I had in my head. How…how did you know?"

He swallowed hard; she could feel it. "I guess I know you better than I thought I did."

She let the tears fall then and studied the drawing. She loved this man, loved everything about him. He *knew* her. She may not know everything about him yet, but she'd find out.

She had to.

Her hand shook once more as she put her finger on the edge of the paper and pressed her lips together. He'd captured almost exactly what she wanted, at least most of it, without even having to ask. Long branches reached out from her right side and across her chest. The trunk of the leafless tree would go down her side, with the roots wrapping around her hips. The bark wouldn't be brown, but a mix of Gaelic symbols in dark black with shadows in between. She might ask him to add splashes of reds and pink in the white parts if it would look good. She wasn't sure. As for the branches, they would tangle together over her breasts with a single hot pink ribbon wrapping itself around them, the edge dangling off the end of a branch. Cherry blossom petals fell down from the tree and added a splash of color to the imagery. At the base of the tree, a rose bush lay with vivid red roses wrapping up her belly and over her scar.

"It's…"

"Your strength and beauty in one. If you don't like the ribbon, we can take it away. Or we can put an octopus or a cake or something on your side."

She snorted. "Really? An octopus? A cake?"

"You're a baker. And people like putting octopuses on their bodies these days. No idea why. Probably because of all the legs."

She wiggled so she sat sideways on his lap. "It's…perfect. I mean, we could add things to it or something, but it's what I wanted. I wanted a tree, I wanted symbols, I wanted pink and red. You *got* me, Sloane. You get me."

He tugged her close and kissed her jaw. "I like to think I get you, Hails. I'll have to sketch your body to make sure I can do this, but you have just the right curves that it won't look like a hunk of bark on your side, you know?"

She grinned. "I trust you, Sloane."

He met her gaze, and something passed over his eyes she couldn't read. "You honor me, Hailey. Fucking honor me."

"I don't think I'd be able to trust anyone else to do this." She hadn't meant to say that, though she'd stated something similar in the past. She felt so raw right now, so open. She trusted him with her ink, but for some reason, she was scared to trust him fully with her heart.

But it was far too late for that fear.

She'd already given it to him.

She had to pray he wouldn't break it.

"I'm selfish enough not to want anyone else to do this," he said, his voice low and gruff. He cleared his throat then, breaking the moment. She didn't blame him. It was so serious, and yet, if she didn't remember to breathe, she'd forget.

"Let's get that trace done," he said after a moment of almost-awkward silence. He helped her off his lap then got the paper ready while she stripped off her shirt and bra. She felt bare, exposed. She'd been far more naked than this, but for some reason, the way he traced her body multiple times reminded her of the hospital. Maybe it was the clinical way he was working with her. While she appreciated it, she wanted her Sloane back.

He paused and frowned. "I'm fucking up."

She shook her head, her eyes clear of tears. She was pulling herself in so there wouldn't be tears. No emotion. Just a raw ache that would never go away.

"You're not."

He let out a sigh and placed the paper and pencil on his table before bringing her into his arms. Her bare chest pressed against his clothed one and she sank into his hold.

"I wanted to keep it professional and not scare you, yet I didn't think about *why* you wanted me to do your ink."

"I wanted you to do my tattoo because I trust you."

"Yeah, to know what you want, to do what you want, but I didn't do what you *need*. You needed me to be a mix of the artist and the boyfriend. And I fucked it up."

She shrugged. "I didn't know that's what I needed."

"Well, I won't fuck it up again." He mumbled something else under his breath, but she didn't quite catch it. "Let's finish up, and I want you standing between my legs as I do it. You feel scared at all, you just touch me." He licked his lips. "Or you could just touch anyway." He leaned back and stripped off his shirt, the sight of his tanned skin, ink, and scars almost too much for her.

She placed her hands on his chest. "Will this hurt with the angle?"

He shook his head. "Nope. If I need you to move a certain way, I'll ask."

He kissed her softly then got to work, this time not clinical at all. It helped her body relax and keep her mind focused on him rather than the odd scenario of being traced for a tattoo that would take multiple sessions and be painful as hell. But she'd made it through the worst pain of her life; she could make it through this.

When he finished, he put his hands on her butt again and brought her closer to him. His lips brushed hers, and she sighed into him, loving his taste. It was a mix of the coffee they'd shared earlier and that unique flavor that was all Sloane.

The kiss started slow, sweet, and oh-so-perfect for what she needed. Then she made a sound in the back of her throat that always seemed to push Sloane right to the edge, and he growled right back.

Perfect.

His hands on her ass tightened and he deepened the kiss, his tongue taking control of hers. He set the pace and she didn't mind it. Not when the outcome was him inside her and her nails raking down his back.

When he pushed her back slightly and stood in front of her, she let her hands run down his chest and hooked them into his belt loops.

"I want my mouth on you, Hails. Think you can stand when I do that?"

She shook her head. "No. The last time you put one of my legs on your shoulder while you had your mouth on my pussy, my knees gave out. Remember?" Her knees about buckled then just thinking about it.

Sloane ran a hand over his beard. "You're right. Okay. I have an idea." He quickly gathered her up, eliciting a squeak from her throat, and moved to the kitchen where he set her down on the island in the middle of his kitchen. It wasn't that big of a kitchen, but the island fit. Barely.

And now her ass was on it.

Nice.

"Isn't this where you cook?" she asked, tilting her head to the side so he could nibble at her neck.

"I've never put food on this. I don't cook all that often. Now stop thinking and let me love you."

She squeezed her eyes shut at his words but let him kiss her, then let him take off her pants. Hailey leaned back on her arms as he knelt in front of her, placing her legs on his shoulders. At the first lick of his tongue on her cunt, she let her head fall back, his name a whisper on her lips.

He devoured her. There wasn't another word for it. The feel of his beard scraping the inside of her thighs made her even wetter—something she hadn't thought possible before Sloane. He hummed along her clit and her legs shook as she came, his name that much louder from her lips.

"Sloane. I need you inside me."

She looked up and he already had his pants off and the condom on his cock. Without a word, he gripped her hips and tugged her to the edge of the island. She sat up to put her hands on his shoulders as he sank into her. He was so freaking big that he stretched her, but it was a good stretch, the kind that led to orgasms and fucking rainbows and unicorns.

When he started to move, she let her head fall back once more. She couldn't breathe, not when her heart raced and her body felt warm, tingly, and on fire all at once. He put his hand on her back and she looked at him.

"I need a better angle," he growled. "Can't feel all of you. Need you to be able to move with me."

With that, he pulled out and carried her over to the living room, one hand fucking her with his fingers, the other keeping her steady. She gripped him tightly, loving this side of him. When he sat on the couch and placed her on top of him, she slid right back on his cock and they both froze. At this angle, he was deep. *So deep.* She had to breathe a moment so she could accommodate all of him.

"You okay, Hails? This good for you?" His voice was low, his eyes dark.

"Yeah," she gasped as she started to rock her hips. "Better than okay. Fuck me, Sloane."

"Then move, darling. *Move.*" He gripped her hips and lifted her up before slamming her back down on his cock. She dug her nails into his shoulders and rode him, their bodies sweat-slick and her pussy clenching him as she neared the edge.

"Come for me, Hails. Come on my cock."

She met his eyes and came, his voice so low it vibrated deep within her. He crushed his mouth to hers as he came with her, his seed hot inside the condom. Her body shook, but she kept moving, not wanting this moment, any moment with him to end.

Because she may have just had another bout of the best sex of her life, but she knew something was still off. There was something wrong with her Sloane.

Something that told her if she didn't figure out what it was, he wouldn't be *her* Sloane for much longer.

Chapter Seven

Sloane stood in the office of Montgomery Ink and tried to figure out what he was going to do next. His back hurt from bending over too long with the last client, on top of not being able to sleep that much the night before.

He hadn't let Hailey spend the night, making sure he took her out to dinner before dropping her off at her place. But he knew she'd caught on that she hadn't woken up in his arms. He'd never woken up with her pressed against him.

There was something wrong with him and he knew it. He had to talk with someone because not doing so would only make things worse. For Hailey.

There wasn't much he could do about how he felt about himself at this point. As soon as he finished her ink, he'd find a way to let her go so she wouldn't end up hurt because of him. Once she knew how he'd come to be, how he'd ended up in Montgomery Ink, she'd see. It wasn't fair to keep at it, to keep having her in his arms. He'd already told himself that he wouldn't sleep with her again—even if his body ached for it. It made him an asshole to keep having her with him, knowing he couldn't keep her. Yes, it was better for Hailey in the long run not to be with a man such as him, but it didn't make it any easier.

"Sloane?" Callie came up to him, her hand on the barely

noticeable bump at her center. "There's a man outside asking for you." She bit her lip. "I don't think he wants to come inside, but I was out there trying to get some fresh air and saw him."

Sloane's senses went on alert. "Who was it? Are you okay? Should you be going outside alone in your condition?"

Callie shook her head, a smile tugging at her lips. "You sound like Morgan. I'm fine going outside in the daylight. I promise. But I don't know his name. He only said he wanted to talk to you." She took a deep breath. "He's wearing a uniform, Sloane. But it's old and dirty. He also looks strung out, but I don't exactly know. It could be that he's homeless and tired, but it seemed a bit more than that."

Sloane froze at her description then cursed. "Don't go outside, Callie. Stay here with Austin and Maya. Okay?"

She frowned at him. "Who is it, Sloane? What has you so worried?"

He lowered his head and kissed her temple. "Just be safe, Callie. I'll go outside and see what it is. If it's a drugged-out guy, though, I don't want you anywhere near him." Nor did he want Hailey anywhere near him, but he couldn't say that without drawing attention to the issue. If Callie were worried about him, she'd bring Hailey over and then he wouldn't be able to hide his past anymore.

And he needed to in order to keep Hailey untainted.

He left a confused Callie in the office and made his way to the front of the store, aware that Maya and Austin were watching him. He ignored them and walked outside in just his Henley, picking up his leather jacket from the hook at the front of the store on his way.

The hauntingly slender man in front of him was a blast from the past. The guy was a few years younger than Sloane, but looked at least fifteen years older. It didn't look like he'd shaved in over a year, nor did it appear as if he'd cut his hair. Normally a buzz cut, it brushed the top of his shoulders and hadn't been washed in far too long.

He wore an old uniform, as well as a threadbare jacket that hadn't belonged to him in the past. He shifted from foot to foot, his attention on the sky above them.

"Jason." Sloane's voice was gruff, but firm. He didn't know why the man was here today, but damn it, it tore at him that Jason was like this.

If it weren't for luck and some determination, he'd be right by Jason's side, living on the street, strung out and in pain.

"Ever wonder what it feels like to fly?" Jason asked, his eyes still on the clouds.

Dread filled Sloane's belly and he did his best to keep his voice calm. "I used to, but I found I like my feet firmly planted on the ground."

Jason met his gaze and Sloane wanted to break down. The man wasn't high, far from it. Instead, his old friend, the man he would have died for, the man he'd almost died for, felt *everything*. There weren't enough drugs in the world to hide the pain of what Jason was feeling—of what Sloane felt every day. Callie had been right in thinking it could be a lack of sleep that led to the look of him, and now Sloane knew that was true. Jason may have used in the past, but it had never been something he constantly did.

"If my feet are on the ground, then I know theirs aren't."

Sloane held back a curse as bile rose in his throat. "They might not have boots on the ground, but we're here, Jason."

"And they aren't. You still dream of them? Still dream of the burning. Because I do. That's why I don't sleep, you see. Because if I sleep, they're louder. Now they're just whispers, telling me I should move on. Telling me I should stay. It doesn't make sense, Sloane. Why doesn't it make any sense?"

Sloane moved forward and slid his leather jacket over Jason's shoulders. It was old enough that Jason might be able to keep it for a bit before it was stolen by someone else on the street. He didn't dare give him something better in case someone thought it was worth Jason's life. He'd done that before and hated seeing the cuts on Jason's lip from the fight. He also could take Jason in or force him off the streets. He'd tried that and had only ended up watching Jason walk away again. His friend *needed* to stay where he was and Sloane could only help so much.

"You need to stay warm, Jason. Have you eaten today? Let me get you something to eat." He wouldn't take him to Taboo, though it was the closest. He didn't want to bring Hailey into this. Or bring this to Hailey. She'd see the darkness beneath his skin and know the truth.

"I can still hear them screaming." Jason faced Sloane fully. "Why did we live? Why did I have to be in the truck behind you guys? I should have been in your truck like normal. But I got in the other one when we ran out of that last building. I got into the wrong one. And now they're dead and I'm here and it doesn't make sense."

Sloane clenched his jaw and put his hand on Jason's shoulder. "Let's get you something to eat, Jason."

The other man shook his head. "I'm okay."

He wasn't. But then again, neither was Sloane. "Let me give you some money for later, then." He pulled out his wallet and took out the rest of the bills he had in there. It wasn't much, but it was something. He stuffed them into the pocket of the jacket he'd given Jason and squeezed the man's shoulder. "Be safe, Jason. Please." Tears pricked at his eyes and he forced them away. He didn't have a right to cry. Not anymore.

"I always am, Sloane. That's the problem. Isn't it?" With that, Jason shuffled off, his hands in his new pockets.

Sloane stood there for another few minutes, watching Jason walk away and knowing he hadn't done enough. He never did.

"Sloane?"

He closed his eyes and took a deep breath, breaking inside once more. Hailey's voice broke him into a thousand pieces, and yet he knew he couldn't show her that. Wouldn't. She'd seen it. What had she heard? What would she do?

"Go inside, Hailey."

He heard her move toward him, but he kept his attention focused on the direction where Jason had disappeared.

"No. I won't. You're cold out here."

"Then you're cold, too. So go inside."

"Sloane." So much depth, so much emotion in that one word.

He wasn't good enough for her. He was too dirty. Too unclean. He'd let the others die. He hadn't been enough. Their deaths slid over his skin as if it owned him. He wasn't what she needed. Regardless that he loved her. He was too rough, too on edge. Too full of guilt and sin.

She wouldn't leave him, not unless he pushed. And if he didn't push, he'd shatter her more. He'd have to break her right then.

"It's over, Hailey. I can't do this anymore. We had our time and it was fun, but I can't do it. We're just too different."

"Look at my face when you say that. Look at my face when you try to end it without telling me anything at all."

He turned then to face her. They stood in the middle of the sidewalk, though it was too cold outside for many people to be out and about. The others in the shop stood at the windows, staring, but he had to get this over with. He had to protect her from him.

"We had what we had, but I'm not made for long term. You're made for so much more than me. So it's over."

She pushed at his chest and growled. "Stop it. Stop acting like this. This isn't who you are."

"I'm exactly this, Hailey." He gripped her wrists and pushed her back. "I'm nothing. Don't you get that? You don't know me at all and that's my fault, but fuck, everything's my fault. So just walk away now."

"You're the one walking away. Not me."

"Then let me walk."

With that, he turned on his heel and headed to the alley that would lead him to the parking lot. He had his wallet and keys and didn't need anything else from the shop. He'd just broken the one woman he'd promised to never hurt, but he hadn't had a choice. If he'd have stayed, she'd have been marred.

He'd let those close to him down before, let them burn and die and scream.

He couldn't do the same to her.

* * * *

Hailey watched him walk away and wondered what the hell had just happened. How could he do that? How could he leave her standing in the middle of the sidewalk as if nothing had happened?

Oh, she'd known he'd do something like this soon, she'd felt it, but she hadn't known it would hurt this much. It shouldn't hurt this much. Right? She rubbed her breastbone and tried to keep the tears from falling. She would not cry. If she did, then it would be final, he'd really be gone and she'd have done nothing about it.

For a moment, an agonizing moment, she thought him leaving was truly about her. Maybe it was about her scars, maybe it was about what he'd seen when he'd traced her. But then she mentally hit herself upside the head and pushed those thoughts away.

Sloane hadn't lied to her about what he felt about her body. He couldn't fake that. And damn it, she'd spent years learning to love herself for who she was and what she'd overcome. She'd be damned if she let herself tear all that away.

He'd left because of something within himself he hadn't been able to run from, hadn't been able to bury deep enough. She knew he'd kept secrets for far too long, had hidden who he was, but she'd thought they'd have longer to figure it all out.

This Jason had been the catalyst for Sloane cutting his ties. She didn't know exactly what had happened, but she'd figure it out...if she could.

From what she could tell, Sloane saw a man within himself that he thought wasn't for her. He'd put her on a damn pedestal and thrown himself into the depths of hell.

She saw a man that was worthy. A man that had fought and come out ahead. He put everything he could into his life and who he was, even if he'd tried to keep his past firmly in the past. Yet the man didn't believe in himself.

"You need to come inside," Maya said from behind her. "It's fucking cold out here, and watching him walk away isn't going to help."

Hailey turned on her heel and wrapped her arms around herself. "He left," she breathed, her voice slightly cracking. "How could he just leave?"

Maya held her arms open, and Hailey moved toward the other woman but not close enough to take the hug.

"If you hug me right now, I'll cry. Be the bitch I know you can be and get ragey with me."

Maya grimaced and tugged on Hailey's arm before dragging her into the shop. "I'll be a bitch in a minute. Let me make sure you don't have freaking frostbite or something."

Callie had a mug in her hand and a frown on her face. "I made you hot cocoa, but it's not as good as when you make it. And I can never get the chocolate shavings right."

Hailey smiled despite herself and took the mug from Callie's hands. "I'm sure it's wonderful. Thank you, Callie." She took a sip and let out a breath. "Sugary," she mumbled. She twisted her mouth. "How many people saw him walk away from me?"

Austin pressed her shoulders and forced her to sit in the front chair. He crouched in front of her, his eyes full of knowing. "Not that many." His voice was deep and reminded her of Sloane's.

She would not cry.

Not now.

Maybe not ever.

If she cried, then she'd break; she'd show she'd given up. And she couldn't do that. Not yet.

"Enough, though," she whispered.

Autumn squeezed in between Austin and the front desk, her eyes wet. "No one's really outside since it's so cold, and no one in Taboo would have been able to see at that angle. So it was just us in the shop. The two clients were in their chairs so they couldn't see either. They're over at Taboo getting a much-needed food break."

"It was just us, Hailey," Callie said softly. "And we're here for you."

Hailey took a sip of the cocoa Callie must have made over at Taboo. Normally, Hailey didn't allow those at Montgomery Ink to work behind the counter, but she didn't have the energy to care about that right then.

"He's an asshole, Hailey," Maya said. "He's an asshole for leaving like he did, but he's *our* asshole. Just think about it, okay? He pushed you away for a reason."

Hailey took another sip. "I know he left for a reason. I know he pushed me away for that same reason. He's just kept that so close to the vest for all these years, it's hard to break through it. I know I shouldn't put him on the same timetable for revealing his secrets as I put myself, but when he does this? Maybe I should have pushed."

Austin let out a breath then squeezed her knee. "Maybe you should have. Maybe *we* should have. Fuck. I've known Sloane for longer than you have, and I still don't know about his past. I don't know the reasons he sometimes takes a week or two off and needs to be alone. I tried to ask once, and he shut me down. I *let* him shut me down. Friends don't do that shit. So you're not alone in this, Hailey."

But she felt alone. She couldn't help it. He hadn't pushed the others away as he had her. She *loved* him, and yet she hadn't been enough to chase away the darkness. If that was even her job to begin with was another story altogether. In fact, she didn't need to chase away all of it, but to function, she needed to *know* of it. That was the difference.

Resolved, she took a deep breath.

"I'm not going to let him go that easily," she said simply. "I'm not that kind of person. Even if we weren't dating, we're friends. I…I can't see him hurting and not want to do something."

"We're here if you need us," Autumn said softly.

"And if you need us to hold him down for you, we can do that, too," Maya added, bringing a smile to Hailey's face.

"I might take you up on that."

"Make sure you make him grovel, though," Maya said with a sad smile. "I mean, after you talk and you're on the right path, make him grovel. Because he hurt you. He might have done it for a reason, but you're hurt and that's not okay."

Hailey pressed her lips together and nodded, tears once again threatening. "You can count on it," she whispered.

Sloane was *hers*, and she'd be damned if anyone took him away from her.

Even him.

Chapter Eight

Sloane wanted a fucking drink but wasn't about to use that to cope. He'd done his best not to when he came home from the desert, and he'd be damned if he did it now. But it was tempting. Damn tempting.

He'd known it was going to hurt like hell when he finally let Hailey go, but he hadn't known it would be this bad. It had only been a day, and yet the agonizing minutes had gone by way too slowly.

He was such a fucking idiot, but there was nothing he could do about it now. He just prayed she'd be okay eventually, and hell, that he hadn't lost his job at Montgomery Ink for leaving like he had.

Seeing Jason like that had ripped him open. He'd bled with that man and had almost died with him. Yet what right did Sloane have to be happier than him? Choices had brought him to the place where he was, but did that mean he deserved the outcome of those choices?

Hailey was far too good for him. She'd survived and thrived. He'd made it through his life, and that wasn't the same. If she were with him, she'd know the truth.

That he was stained with the blood of his fallen men. That he'd killed to protect them, but hadn't done a good enough job. He'd killed to protect himself and his men, yet how could he live with that? He hadn't been enough for the others and yet somehow he'd lived.

He wasn't going to end it—that wasn't the kind of man he was—but he also couldn't consciously bring another down with him.

Hailey deserved better than that. Deserved better than him.

The knock on the door surprised him, but it shouldn't have. It was probably Austin here to kick his ass for leaving not only Hailey but also the shop. The big man could probably take him, and that was saying something.

Without bothering to look out the peephole, he opened the door and froze.

"Hailey," he said, his voice a broken growl.

She had her hands folded over her chest and a glare on her face. She looked hot as hell and even madder.

"If you shut the door in my face, I'll just keep knocking, so you better let me in."

Caught off guard and a little turned on, he moved to the side so she could storm past. And storm she did. She let out a small growl and turned on her heel.

"Well? Close the door, Sloane. We have to talk."

He'd done his talking in front of Montgomery Ink. If he did it again, he wasn't sure what he'd say.

"I already said what I needed to."

"Well fuck you, Sloane Gordon. You need to let *me* talk, then. And when I'm done, you better be ready to talk or I'm going to kick your ass."

His eyes widened, but he didn't say anything. He'd never seen her like this, but damn if he didn't like it. He'd loved her passion before, but hell, this was something more.

He finally closed the door, and she lifted her chin. Before he could take a step toward her—or away from her since his mind couldn't figure it out—she stripped off her top so he could see her scars. He froze, unable to speak, to think. Her face was one of fury, but her stance that of strength.

"You see this? This is all of me. I'm not going anywhere. You think I'm less of a woman because of what happened to me? You think I'm less of a person? I sure as hell don't think you're any less of a man because you have PTSD, are scarred, or had to go through hell. You need to talk to me. You got it? You need to tell me what is going on in that head of yours and know I'm going to be there. I was your friend before this and I'm not going away."

Sloane opened his mouth to speak but couldn't formulate words.

"I don't know what happened over there because you won't tell me. If you don't want to go into the details, that's fine. For now. Because you need to talk about it, Sloane. Hiding away from it clearly isn't helping. I love you, Sloane, and you're in pain. I hate to see it and yet there's nothing I can do if you keep hiding. So, yeah, I'm standing here topless so you can see every inch of my pain, of my past. I'm not hiding anymore. Please don't hide from me."

Shame covered him and Sloane took a step forward. He didn't touch her, couldn't if he wanted to think, but he let out a shuddering breath.

He hadn't missed that she'd told him she loved him. But could she love him without knowing the truth? He walked past her to the couch and heard the telltale sign of a sob. Fuck. He was messing this up.

When he pulled the throw off the couch and wrapped it around her shoulders, she frowned at him. "I don't want you to get cold."

"I don't feel much of anything, Sloane."

He closed his eyes and took a deep breath. She was here. Here and waiting. If he didn't open himself up, she'd leave for good, and he'd always know he'd hurt her, scared her. Yet once he told her everything, she might leave anyway.

But what way would hurt her less?

"I've killed, Hailey." He cleared his throat. "I've killed and hurt. I've watched the life drain out of someone's eyes because I was ordered to. Because if I didn't, they'd kill my men or me. I didn't want to, never did, but I did it anyway."

She pressed her lips together. "I figured you had, Sloane. That doesn't change what I think of you."

"It should, damn it." He paced, running a hand over his head. Hair was just starting to scrape his palm and he knew he needed to shave again. That didn't matter, though. The only thing that mattered was making sure Hailey understood what he was saying, understood *why* he'd left her standing on the street like he had.

"I'm dirty, Hailey. I have blood on my hands that I'll never wash off. No matter how many times I told the shrinks after I got out, they didn't understand. The only ones that do are the ones that were over there with me." He stopped pacing and met her gaze. "But out of all the men I went over there with, the only one that came back was Jason. And you saw him. He's what I should be."

"Don't say that. You know you're not supposed to be that shadow."

He shook his head and let out a shout. "I damn well should. I lost *everyone* but Jason over there, and fuck it, I lost Jason there, too. He didn't come back whole, no one did, but for some reason I came back with more than I should. How could I? That roadside bomb wiped out my unit. Fucking burned them to a crisp and I was forced to listen to it, to watch it. I almost bled out and burned with them, but I didn't. Instead, I have to walk in this world every damn day knowing I'm not good enough. No matter what I do, I'll never be worth it. I'll have never earned my life. Jason didn't die that day either, yet he left more on the field than I did."

"Sloane." Tears slid down her cheeks, but he didn't wipe them away like he normally would have. If he did, he'd break, and he was already shattered as it was.

"Yes, I have PTSD. That doesn't go away with the love of a good woman, with the ability to *see* that I have it. It's never going to go away, Hailey. I might be able to look like I'm normal on most days, but sometimes I'm going to freak the fuck out. Sometimes I'm going to have nightmares. Sometimes I'm not going to be okay. How is that good enough for you? How can you stand to be with me knowing I'm not whole? I came home. Others didn't. My friends had to die for me to be able to stand here in front of you. They were the ones that didn't make it and yet because they died, I lived. I was able to make it out and yet their families will never know how much they meant to me."

She choked out a sob. "I'm not normal, Sloane. I'm sure as hell not whole. You said yourself I was more than my scars, and yet you don't think you are as well? Scars aren't just the ones on our skin, aren't just what we can see when we look in the mirror. I *know* I have them inside, on my heart, on my soul. I *know* you have them, too. And I'm fine with it. I love the man in front of me, scars and all. Can't you love him, too?"

"I'll taint you," he whispered.

"You can't, Sloane. Just love me. Love is enough to get us started. We can talk to someone if we need to, but love *is* enough. It doesn't heal all wounds, doesn't make the past go away. It doesn't heal our scars, doesn't erase the pain, but it *does* make it worth it. With you, I know I'm okay. I know I'm loved. Even if you haven't said it."

He let out a breath then stepped toward her. She cupped his face with one hand, the other on the blanket before he cupped her face instead. When she wiped the tears from his face he hadn't known had fallen, he closed his eyes.

"I love you, Hailey. I love all of you, every breath of you, every ounce of your soul. But I'm not worthy of you."

"You're a fool, but I love you, too, Sloane. And you don't get to decide if you're worthy of me. That's not how love works. You don't get to walk away from me, leave me bleeding and in agony because you're afraid to hurt me. You *hurt* me anyway, trying to protect me, and I'm not going to let you do that again. You hear me? If you want to leave me, then you do it without lying to me. You do it by saying you don't love me and you don't want me."

He opened his eyes and cursed. "I love you, Hailey. I just damn well said it. Of course, I want you. I can't breathe with wanting you."

"Then let that be enough. We can do anything, Sloane. But we have to be together to persevere. You're a good man, Sloane Gordon. I saw you with Jason. I saw you try to help and know you could only do so much. Don't become him, Sloane. Help him, but don't let his pain take away what you have. Don't fade into the shadows because you feel you should. Step into the light *because* of those you lost. Show them that their loss was worth it. Show the world that you made it and you live for them, not in spite of them."

Jesus, he loved this woman. She saw into the heart of him and yet he'd almost lost it all because he was so scared.

"I love you, Hails. I pushed you away before I had you, then did again because I was scared."

"Don't do it again," she whispered, tears sliding down her cheeks in earnest. He wiped them away with his thumbs.

"I fucked up."

"Yeah, you did," she said honestly.

He snorted.

"Don't do it again. You don't get to push me away because you're scared."

He kissed her then, softly, with everything he had within himself. She kissed him back, and he fell that much more in love with her.

He pulled away and traced one finger down her side and under her breast. "Don't hide from me either. I know you haven't, but..."

"But I might. Because it's scary. I know." She kissed his chest. "I promise to be open."

"I'll never leave you again," he said softly.

"I want to believe that," she whispered. "So prove it to me, Sloane. Every day. Prove it to me."

"Be with me. We've hidden everything else in the past, but I'm all me now. You're all you. We're bare. You got it? You're mine. I fucked up, but I'm not doing it again. I'm going to have you every way I can and I'm not letting go."

She smiled softly and nodded. "We've wasted too many years because we were scared. I'm not going to waste any more."

He kissed her then, this time deeper. "I love you, Hails."

"I love you, too. Oh, and happy Valentine's Day."

He frowned and thought about the day before letting out a rough chuckle. "Happy Valentine's Day, baby."

She let the blanket fall from her fingers and he let out a groan. He hadn't allowed himself to look at her fully before, but now he took her all in. When she licked her lips, he had to have her.

He crushed his mouth to hers even as she tugged on his shirt. Soon they were stripped down, pressing their bodies together as tightly as possible, hands roaming and grasping. He pulled out a condom from his discarded pants pocket and let her slide it over him. The act almost made him come, but he held strong. Barely. He moved her toward the front door and gripped her thighs.

"I've wanted to fuck you hard against a door since the first time," he growled.

She bit his lip and opened for him. When he slid inside oh-so-slowly, they both moaned.

"Is it still fucking when we love each other? Or is it making love?" Her nails dug into his shoulder and he slowly pumped in and out of her.

"I know it's making love when it's slow." He sped up. "When it's going fast,"—he pounded into her—"when it's me fucking you hard. It's fucking, loving, and everything in between."

She bit into her lip and rode him even as he fucked her into the door, their bodies sweat-slick and their moans rising. When her cunt clamped around him and her eyes darkened, he slammed into her, coming hard with her. He kissed her lips, his body shaking. She kissed him back.

"Love you, Hails. All of you." He wrapped his arms around her, knowing he'd have to take them down to the floor soon before his legs gave out.

She nipped at his chin, her hands lazily skimming his back. "Love you, too, Sloane. You're my broody, bearded, inked man. What more could I want?"

With her in his arms, in his heart, he knew the answer. Life. And she was it. He wouldn't run from her anymore. He couldn't. She'd seen the heart of him and hadn't run, hadn't shied away.

He'd been wrong before, but now he was all too right.

He had his life, his future in his arms.

He didn't need anything else.

He'd found his future in the one person he'd hidden from.

He'd found his Hailey.

Epilogue

Hailey winced as the needle dug into her skin, but she didn't call out. Tattoos were not for wimps, that was for sure. Yeah, the nice adrenaline rush that came from long-term sessions under the needle were nice, but hell, it *hurt*.

But it would be worth it in the end.

Plus, her tattoo artist was sexy as hell and pretty damn gentle, all things considered.

They were on the final session for her ink and she had the routine down by now. Sloane had curtained off his station so it was only the two of them, though she'd allowed Autumn, Maya, Callie, and even Austin to come in and look. The latter hadn't made Sloane happy at first, but he'd relented. They'd wanted to make sure she had support during not only the long and painful sessions but also during the emotional waves that came with it.

Sloane wasn't tattooing nipples on her skin.

He was tattooing memories.

With each new detail, she saw the strength she'd needed, saw the pain and agony she'd faced, saw the tears she'd let fall. It wasn't easy to let the others see what had become of her chest, but they hadn't treated her any differently. She wasn't made of glass, but of hardcore power and woman.

And that she was okay with.

They'd embarked on a journey she hadn't thought possible.

She'd hidden her scars, her past from him, from the world, and yet now, everything was out in the open and she didn't feel any less.

In fact, she felt like she had *more*.

Every time she looked in the mirror now, she wouldn't see a survivor—but a woman with a future, a woman with a past, a woman with a man she loved who'd inked her skin with such tender care, she knew he'd put part of himself into each stroke.

"It's magnificent," Maya said softly, unlike how the other woman usually spoke. Of course, Maya was going through her own hell right then—not that she'd talk about it with Hailey. Now that Hailey had found her future, though, she knew she was steady enough to help Maya. If and when the other woman let her in, she'd be there for her.

"I do good ink," Sloane said simply as he finished up part of the color shading on the inside of the trunk.

She winced when he went over the same area for the fourth time, but didn't call out. She was getting the hang of this tattoo thing. Maybe next time she'd go a bit smaller, though.

"You do better than good ink," Maya said. "It's a fucking masterpiece. I have to say I was a bit jealous at first that he was the one to do this for you, but hell, I don't think I could have done this justice. Not in the way he's doing it."

Hailey let a single tear fall. "He's amazing."

"I am," Sloane said with a smile.

Maya snorted. "He's putting his love for you in the ink, so yeah, it's perfect. I can't wait to see it when it's all healed." She leaned down and brushed a kiss to Hailey's temple, surprising them both. "I'll leave you two alone for the last bit. Thanks for letting me watch."

Hailey frowned as the other woman left them, but Sloane clucked his tongue. "When Maya is ready to talk, she will." He wiped down Hailey's side, then patted her thigh. "I'm all done, baby. I don't want you to stand yet since I want you to drink some juice first, but I can bring the mirror over."

She smiled and held out her hand. "Kiss me before you do. I want your lips on mine before I look."

Sloane moved around to the front of the bench then lowered his head to hers. She kept her eyes open so she could watch his face.

"I love you, Sloane. Every inch of you."

"Same goes, Hails. Same goes. Love you, baby."

She'd look at her new tattoo in full later when she could breathe, but first she'd look at the man she'd fallen for, the man who had fallen for her.

Hailey had been so scared to move forward with him, so scared to do more than survive, but now, with Sloane in her life and her own head on straight, she had more than she could ever hope for.

The two of them had been through their own hells and had come out the other side stronger than ever—scarred, broken, but *alive*.

They'd hidden their pasts, yet opened up to one another to ensure that they'd move on together. Her ink would be hidden from most, but not from him, not from the man she loved.

He was inked on her skin, on her soul, on her heart.

He was hers.

Forever.

* * * *

Also from 1001 Dark Nights and Carrie Ann Ryan, discover Wicked Wolf: A Redwood Pack Novella.

Discover 1001 Dark Nights Collection Three

HIDDEN INK by Carrie Ann Ryan
A Montgomery Ink Novella

BLOOD ON THE BAYOU by Heather Graham
A Cafferty & Quinn Novella

SEARCHING FOR MINE by Jennifer Probst
A Searching For Novella

DANCE OF DESIRE by Christopher Rice

ROUGH RHYTHM by Tessa Bailey
A Made In Jersey Novella

DEVOTED by Lexi Blake
A Masters and Mercenaries Novella

Z by Larissa Ione
A Demonica Underworld Novella

FALLING UNDER YOU by Laurelin Paige
A Fixed Trilogy Novella

EASY FOR KEEPS by Kristen Proby
A Boudreaux Novella

UNCHAINED by Elisabeth Naughton
An Eternal Guardians Novella

HARD TO SERVE by Laura Kaye
A Hard Ink Novella

DRAGON FEVER by Donna Grant
A Dark Kings Novella

KAYDEN/SIMON by Alexandra Ivy/Laura Wright
A Bayou Heat Novella

STRUNG UP by Lorelei James
A Blacktop Cowboys® Novella

MIDNIGHT UNTAMED by Lara Adrian
A Midnight Breed Novella

TRICKED by Rebecca Zanetti
A Dark Protectors Novella

DIRTY WICKED by Shayla Black
A Wicked Lovers Novella

A SEDUCTIVE INVITATION by Lauren Blakely
A Seductive Nights New York Novella

SWEET SURRENDER by Liliana Hart
A MacKenzie Family Novella

For more information, visit 1001DarkNights.com.

Discover 1001 Dark Nights Collection Two

WICKED WOLF by Carrie Ann Ryan
WHEN IRISH EYES ARE HAUNTING by Heather Graham
EASY WITH YOU by Kristen Proby
MASTER OF FREEDOM by Cherise Sinclair
CARESS OF PLEASURE by Julie Kenner
ADORED by Lexi Blake
HADES by Larissa Ione
RAVAGED by Elisabeth Naughton
DREAM OF YOU by Jennifer L. Armentrout
STRIPPED DOWN by Lorelei James
RAGE/KILLIAN by Alexandra Ivy/Laura Wright
DRAGON KING by Donna Grant
PURE WICKED by Shayla Black
HARD AS STEEL by Laura Kaye
STROKE OF MIDNIGHT by Lara Adrian
ALL HALLOWS EVE by Heather Graham
KISS THE FLAME by Christopher Rice
DARING HER LOVE by Melissa Foster
TEASED by Rebecca Zanetti
THE PROMISE OF SURRENDER by Liliana Hart

Also from 1001 Dark Nights

THE SURRENDER GATE By Christopher Rice
SERVICING THE TARGET By Cherise Sinclair

For more information, visit 1001DarkNights.com.

Discover 1001 Dark Nights Collection One

FOREVER WICKED by Shayla Black
CRIMSON TWILIGHT by Heather Graham
CAPTURED IN SURRENDER by Liliana Hart
SILENT BITE: A SCANGUARDS WEDDING by Tina Folsom
DUNGEON GAMES by Lexi Blake
AZAGOTH by Larissa Ione
NEED YOU NOW by Lisa Renee Jones
SHOW ME, BABY by Cherise Sinclair
ROPED IN by Lorelei James
TEMPTED BY MIDNIGHT by Lara Adrian
THE FLAME by Christopher Rice
CARESS OF DARKNESS by Julie Kenner

Also from 1001 Dark Nights

TAME ME by J. Kenner

For more information, visit 1001DarkNights.com.

About Carrie Ann Ryan

New York Times and USA Today Bestselling Author Carrie Ann Ryan never thought she'd be a writer. Not really. No, she loved math and science and even went on to graduate school in chemistry. Yes, she read as a kid and devoured teen fiction and Harry Potter, but it wasn't until someone handed her a romance book in her late teens that she realized that there was something out there just for her. When another author suggested she use the voices in her head for good and not evil, The Redwood Pack and all her other stories were born.

Carrie Ann is a bestselling author of over twenty novels and novellas and has so much more on her mind (and on her spreadsheets *grins*) that she isn't planning on giving up her dream anytime soon.

www.CarrieAnnRyan.com

Wicked Wolf
A Redwood Pack Novella
By Carrie Ann Ryan

The war between the Redwood Pack and the Centrals is one of wolf legend. Gina Eaton lost both of her parents when a member of their Pack betrayed them. Adopted by the Alpha of the Pack as a child, Gina grew up within the royal family to become an enforcer and protector of her den. She's always known fate can be a tricky and deceitful entity, but when she finds the one man that could be her mate, she might throw caution to the wind and follow the path set out for her, rather than forging one of her own.

Quinn Weston's mate walked out on him five years ago, severing their bond in the most brutal fashion. She not only left him a shattered shadow of himself, but their newborn son as well. Now, as the lieutenant of the Talon Pack's Alpha, he puts his whole being into two things: the safety of his Pack and his son.

When the two Alphas put Gina and Quinn together to find a way to ensure their treaties remain strong, fate has a plan of its own. Neither knows what will come of the Pack's alliance, let alone one between the two of them. The past paved their paths in blood and heartache, but it will take the strength of a promise and iron will to find their future.

* * * *

There were times to drool over a sexy wolf.

Sitting in the middle of a war room disguised as a board meeting was not one of those times.

Gina Jamenson did her best not to stare at the dark-haired, dark-eyed man across the room. The hint of ink peeking out from under his shirt made her want to pant. She *loved* ink and this wolf clearly had a lot of it. Her own wolf within nudged at her, a soft brush beneath her skin, but she ignored her. When her wolf whimpered, Gina promised herself that she'd go on a long run in the forest later. She didn't understand why her wolf was acting like this, but she'd deal with it when she was in a better place. She just couldn't let her wolf have control right then—even for a man such as the gorgeous specimen a mere ten feet from her.

Today was more important than the wants and feelings of a half wolf, half witch hybrid.

Today was the start of a new beginning.

At least that's what her dad had told her.

Considering her father was also the Alpha of the Redwood Pack, he would be in the know. She'd been adopted into the family when she'd been a young girl. A rogue wolf during the war had killed her parents, setting off a long line of events that had changed her life.

As it was, Gina wasn't quite sure how she'd ended up in the meeting between the two Packs, the Redwoods and the Talons. Sure, the Packs had met before over the past fifteen years of their treaty, but this meeting seemed different.

This one seemed more important somehow.

And they'd invited—more like *demanded*—Gina to attend.

At twenty-six, she knew she was the youngest wolf in the room by far. Most of the wolves were around her father's age, somewhere in the hundreds. The dark-eyed wolf might have been slightly younger than that, but only slightly if the power radiating off of him was any indication.

Wolves lived a long, long time. She'd heard stories of her people living into their thousands, but she'd never met any of the wolves who had. The oldest wolf she'd met was a friend of the family, Emeline, who was over five hundred. That number boggled her mind even though she'd grown up knowing the things that went bump in the night were real.

Actually, she *was* one of the things that went bump in the night.

"Are we ready to begin?" Gideon, the Talon Alpha, asked, his voice low. It held that dangerous edge that spoke of power and authority.

Her wolf didn't react the way most wolves would, head and eyes down, shoulders dropped. Maybe if she'd been a weaker wolf, she'd have bowed to his power, but as it was, her wolf was firmly entrenched within the Redwoods. Plus, it wasn't as if Gideon was *trying* to make her bow just then. No, those words had simply been spoken in his own voice.

Commanding without even trying.

Then again, he *was* an Alpha.

Kade, her father, looked around the room at each of his wolves and nodded. "Yes. It is time."

Their formality intrigued her. Yes, they were two Alphas who held a treaty and worked together in times of war, but she had thought they were also friends.

Maybe today was even more important than she'd realized.

Gideon released a sigh that spoke of years of angst and worries. She didn't know the history of the Talons as well as she probably should have, so she didn't know exactly why there was always an air of sadness and pain around the Alpha.

Maybe after this meeting, she'd be able to find out more.

Of course, in doing so, she'd have to *not* look at a certain wolf in the corner. His gaze was so intense she was sure he was studying her. She felt it down in her bones, like a fiery caress that promised something more.

Or maybe she was just going crazy and needed to find a wolf to scratch the itch.

She might not be looking for a mate, but she wouldn't say no to something else. Wolves were tactile creatures after all.

"Gina?"

She blinked at the sound of Kade's voice and turned to him.

She was the only one standing other than the two wolves in charge of security—her uncle Adam, the Enforcer, and the dark-eyed wolf.

Well, *that* was embarrassing.

On behalf of 1001 Dark Nights,
Liz Berry and M.J. Rose would like to thank ~

Steve Berry
Doug Scofield
Kim Guidroz
Jillian Stein
InkSlinger PR
Dan Slater
Asha Hossain
Chris Graham
Pamela Jamison
Jessica Johns
Dylan Stockton
Richard Blake
BookTrib After Dark
The Dinner Party Show
and Simon Lipskar

15979602R00074

Printed in Great Britain
by Amazon